Flare Up

Adele Jones

Flare Up

A novella
Copyright © Adele Jones, 2025
Cover design by Kirsten Hart.
Dumbbell icon by Flaticon.
Layout by Adele Jones.
ISBN: 978-1-7640451-0-0

Published by Adele Jones
Author, 2025
Toowoomba QLD 4350
Australia
adelejonesauthor.com.au

National library of Australia Cataloguing-in-Publication Information:

A catalogue record for this
Work is available from the
National Library of Australia

This is a work of fiction. The story, all names, characters, and incidents portrayed in this production are fictious. No identification with actual persons, living or deceased, places, buildings, and products is intended or should be inferred.

This novella uses Australian style conventions for spelling, punctuation, grammar and Australian terminology.

Chapter 1

'Jetto, you've been eyeballing that poster for weeks, man. Just do it.'

Jett dragged his eyes from the bodybuilding comp advertisement and dropped his sweat-drenched towel onto the bench, next to his kit bag. 'I couldn't make big enough gains, Luca. Not before the comp.'

He restrained a grimace when the gym manager's mouth twitched upward. Luca's smirk made Jett feel like he was stepping barefoot on snails. The dank scent of urinals and wet cement leaked through the communal space dividing the men's toilets and showers.

'I could help you make those gains.' Luca leaned against the gym lockers, which stood like silent spectators behind them. His eyes ran over Jett's body. 'You'd still have to work hard and give up your ice cream addiction, but you'd come up killer ripped. You're pretty cut—for a kid.'

Grabbing fresh jocks, shorts, and a towel from his bag, Jett zipped it up extra fast. 'I'm not getting involved in that, Luca.'

'The big T's your best friend, man. If you don't overdo it, no one'll know. But I'm not talking about the T.'

'Not interested. Ever.'

Luca closed the distance between them and a muscle flinched at his jaw. Jett offered an indifferent shrug, as if the man's space invasion didn't bother him. He might only be eighteen, but he wasn't going to be bullied into doing something dumb—and Luca had been acting weird these past weeks, even for Luca. Since his appointment as gym manager six months back, the man had gone from over-the-top-body-worshipper to something more ... menacing.

Jett refused to back away, even though he could feel heat radiating off the man. 'Luca, what you're doing is illegal.'

Luca scoffed and patted Jett's chest with the flat of his palm. 'You and I both know you're a nice "churchy" boy, Jetto—and I don't mean the school. You're not going to say anything.'

Of *course*, Luca would pull that line. Teeth gritted, Jett turned away. As he did, a weird flash in Luca's eyes caught his attention. It was a rippling fluorescent glow, with a rim of reflected colours, like those off an oil slick on water. He couldn't resist glancing back, but the only thing eyeballing him was irritation. *Must be the dodgy lights in here.* He escaped to the showers.

Luca was gone when Jett got out. He towelled off his hair, doused himself with body spray and pulled on a fresh muscle shirt. Running some product through his blond hair, he left it to dry in a funky-messy style. Stuffing everything back in his kit, he exited the locker-room— right into a swarm of people exiting a jump fit class.

'Hi, Jett.'

He swivelled towards the voices and found three girls about his age checking him out.

'Uh … hi.' He had no idea who they were or how they knew his name, but at his reply they leaned into each other and giggled. Casually, one of them lifted her shirt to wipe sweat from her face, revealing her sports bra. He ducked his head and kept walking.

Heading for his car, he passed the glass walls of the workout room. The clank of weights being locked onto bench-stands echoed through the corridor. In the far corner, Luca was spotting for another training buddy. Jett tried not to gawk at the other guy's gains since he'd last seen him. One week. *How?* His gym mate wasn't even lifting half Jett's PBs but was bulking like a gorilla. It didn't seem possible.

He shut down the thought. The competition was only four months away. No way could he do it.

He slid on a pair of sunglasses as he exited the building to filter the sunrays streaking the azure dome above. The Queensland sun rarely disappointed, its brilliance making the metallic paintwork of his blue Mazda luminesce. He unlocked the car, dumped his kit in the back, and sank into a cocoon of heat.

Turning over the engine, he cranked the aircon. Although it was still spring for another week, the weather was already ramping up in anticipation of summer. That meant Dad would do most of their meal prep on the barbeque outside so they could make the most of hot, lazy evenings. And by the turn of season, they'd be even closer to the waterfront, offering unobstructed views of Moreton Bay from their house.

Jett hummed along to the stereo as he cruised home. As usual, his twin sister, Sophie, had left her preferred selection of pop artists running. She was the brains, he was the brawn, and given they co-owned the car, he couldn't complain too loudly about her playlist, but her track selection was more boy band than his preferred style. Their parents assured him there'd been no mix up at the hospital, despite her taste in music being seriously questionable. Halfway through the first song, he flicked to a radio station playing a song with a base that pounded through his body.

It wasn't long before he pulled into the driveway of their house. He left the comfort of the car and entered a zone of chaos. His mother's voice reached him from an undisclosed room.

'Anna, you need to sort your toys before we pack up your room. You don't even play with half of them anymore.'

Good luck with that, Mum. Dad was conspicuously absent, working late likely, or some other excuse to escape Mum's crazy 'move in under a week' mood—and they were only at day two. His parents had explained there was a tight overlap between settlement and a contract clause stating the house must be vacated by a given date. Not only would they be required to pay rent daily if they continued occupancy beyond that, but they would also have to pay for the new owner's temporary accommodation and any additional costs incurred.

Jett could tell from Dad's reaction he hadn't expected Mum to embrace this timeline with such enthusiasm, but her logic went beyond financial benefits. She claimed moving fast meant she could also save her annual leave for Christmas and New Year's, to enjoy being together in their new home. Thinking the quiet part he'd never say out loud, Jett would rather hide with Dad than subject himself to this hyper-moving frenzy.

He dumped his kit at the base of the stairs and headed for the kitchen. He'd just opened the freezer door when Sophie breezed in behind him.

'Don't bother. Anna ate the last of your ice cream after school.' She laughed at his groan. He had to be quick to beat their younger sister to his stash. 'With school winding down towards Christmas break, I think she's getting in the holiday vibe early.'

'Man. She seriously owes me. I totally smashed myself at the gym, *after* slogging it out at work.' He slapped the door closed and jogged through the house. Collecting his bag, he took the steps to the second floor two at a time. Dodging stacks of boxes on the upstairs landing, he tossed the kit on his bed and returned to the hall.

Outside the glitter-covered door of his little sister's room, he growled, 'Anna?'

A giggle emanated from within. Jett smothered his own laughter. He barged into the bedroom. The nine-year-old girl was poised for action, cat-like, on the bed, in a mound of stuffed toys and dolls.

'Ice cream thief.' Jett feigned a lunge in her direction. Anna squealed and jumped off the bed. Allowing her a slight head start, he swiftly reeled her in, then hauled her over his shoulder. 'And now we return to the scene of the crime.'

He stomped along the hall with Anna laughing hysterically. Marching down the stairs and to the kitchen, he deposited her in front of the refrigerator. Pulling open the freezer door, he gestured to the empty space where the ice cream container had been and raised his eyebrows.

'It was my goldfish.'

'Goldy died. *Two* months ago.'

'It was ... Sophie.'

'Not,' echoed from a distant room.

'It was—' She crab-stepped and ran. '—me!'

'That's it, you owe me an ice cream date, Anna.' Jett laughed as she chortled all the way back to her room. It was no threat at all. He always paid.

Settling for a protein shake, he made a fresh suspension of his go-to powder and sipped on it as he returned to his room. Opening his kit, he pulled out his sweat-soaked gym gear and filthy work clothes. A phone rang in the house somewhere. Sophie's ring tone. It was probably Blaine. His sister's kind-of-boyfriend was his best mate, but lately Jett heard most of Blaine's news second-hand. It had been weeks since they'd last caught up.

He dropped his clothes in the dirty clothes hamper and pretended not to see Anna creep into the room and hunch behind his bed. As he lifted the hamper to take it to the laundry, she jumped up and shrieked, 'Got you.'

He shouted in 'fright' and tossed his load in the air. 'I'll have to start calling you stealth pilot, Anna,' he teased, collecting the clothes strewn across the floor.

'Have you got a headache?'

Jett frowned in question as Anna picked a small, clip-seal bag out of his kit bag. At the same moment, Sophie barged into his room.

'They've asked me to cover a shift at the restaurant tonight. You don't need our car?' She stopped and stared at Anna, who was holding up the bag and staring at the three capsules in it. Sophie's eyes narrowed in suspicion.

'Where did you get those, Anna?'

'Jett's gym bag.'

'No kidding.'

Jett heard the accusation in his twin's voice as her gaze cut to him. He ground his teeth and growled, 'Luca.'

'Your overzealous gym manager?'

He reached across and took the pills from Anna. The words 'take one a day, if you're game' were written in small-print permanent ink across the packet. 'He's being an idiot. That's all.' Taking aim, he lobbed the small bag into the nearby bin. *Swish.* '*That's* where they belong. Yeah, Soph, car's all yours. Keys are on the key hook. Anna, we'll have our ice cream date another time.'

Sophie backed from the room without another word while Anna 'aw'ed her disappointment. Jett could tell his twin wasn't sure what to believe. Whatever was up with Luca lately, he'd seriously crossed the line this time. Sophie would say report him, but even if that report was only to the gym owners, Jett knew it would mean a whole bunch of fuss he'd rather avoid, not to mention finding a new gym. Worse, if Luca wasn't caught, he'd circulate discrediting rumours Jett would then have to deflect. Those rumours would make it a case of Luca's word against his.

He shook his head. Luca was right about him being too nice to rat him out. But how long could he turn a blind eye?

Chapter 2

Jett groaned as his phone alarm throttled the pre-dawn silence. He turned it off, rubbed his eyes, and dragged back the bedcovers. He'd spent hours online the previous night searching for training programs that might get him over the line, *if* he decided to go for the bodybuilding comp. It wasn't like he *had* to do it, but the challenge intrigued him. His training partners told him he had the perfect genetics for bodybuilding, and it wasn't like he was starting from scratch.

Opening the wardrobe door, he pulled out a set of work clothes. The high-visibility stripes made his uniform easy to locate, even in shadows. As he closed the wardrobe he noticed a different glow—from his bin. What the—?

He rifled through the trash. Near the bottom he found the source of light. It was the capsules from Luca.

Their luminescence forced him to squint. *What on earth* is *that stuff?* Either Luca was playing some sort of joke or the manager's steroid supplier had taken him for a ride. An image pushed into Jett's mind—the glow in

Luca's eyes. It was the exact same rippling hues, over a predominantly green base. Maybe he hadn't been seeing things?

Jett shoved the bag with the capsules into the top drawer of his desk and headed for the kitchen. Those questions would have to wait. He couldn't afford to be late.

Soon he had eggs poaching on the stove top. He loaded them with asparagus, quinoa and capsicum. While waiting, he pulled his pre-prepared meals from the fridge, jostled the containers into his lunchbox, and placed it on the counter bench. His workmates joked about having to tie up their dogs in case he ate them too, along with his twice-weekly cook-offs. 'You'll ruin the sheilas for us, Jetto.' As an apprentice, he didn't expect anything less than their mockery.

Sophie staggered into the kitchen and folded onto a chair with a groan. 'Morning, Jett. But note I did *not* say "good".'

'What're you doing up this early?'

'There's a compulsory info session this morning for that summer placement program I'm doing. Afterwards, I'm meeting some friends in the city to celebrate finishing first year. But Mum's decided she wants to start moving the non-essentials *now*. So, I'm box filling, then catching the train in. *Conveniently*, Dad has an early videoconference scheduled, so he won't be "available" to help.' She drew invisible quotation marks in the air with her fingers. Sophie closed her eyes, slumped lower in her chair, and moaned. 'Coffee. It's all I ask.'

'You should try some of this, Soph. Best stuff for keeping you lean and mean, but it sounds like you'll need no help with the "mean" today.' He laughed as his sister, with eyes still closed, extended her fist in a pathetic effort at hitting him. 'I'm guessing Dad's still in the doghouse for messing up Mum's moving plan with his inefficient packing approach?'

'Uh-huh. Poor Dad. He's never been good with spatial stuff, just numbers. Which leaves more packing for moi, whee ... Can't wait for the post-move cleaning.'

'How 'bout I call Blaine and ask him to come around to help you? Bet you'd muster up some enthusiasm then.'

'Shut up.' Sophie scrunched up her face, but immediately assumed a sappy smile.

Jett turned off the stove element, chanting, 'Blaine and Sophie sitting in a tree, k-i double-s i-n-g.' A fist pounded into his shoulder. 'Ouch!'

He turned to find his twin at his side.

'Coffee. You're in my way, fit boy.'

Jett stepped aside so she could access the coffee machine. Sophie positioned a cup under the spout and pressed start, while he lifted his breakfast from the pan onto a large plate. The machine sputtered and spat as he sat at the table and began eating. Shortly, his twin slouched into the chair opposite him, hands cupping her mug like an ancient woman guarding the syrup of youth.

'Okay, what's with the drugs in your bag? 'Cause they sure weren't headache pills.'

Jett stopped mid-cut and levelled his gaze on her. 'Like I said, Luca put them there. He saw me looking at a bodybuilding comp and tried convincing me I could make enough gains if I took some new thing he's promoting. Heard him banging on about a supplement with some guys I train with, so I'm guessing that's what it is. I didn't know he'd put some in my bag while I was in the shower though.'

He ignored the arch of Sophie's brow as she assessed his claim.

'I dunno what the pills are, but I wouldn't do that. You might be the smart one of the dynamic duo, but you know I'm not *that* dumb, right?'

Sophie frowned at him over the mug mouth, which she was now holding at nose level, as if the smell alone could restore vigour. 'You're not stupid. We've had that conversation. You're just too nice. But bodybuilding? As in "itsy-bitsy, teeny-weeny, yellow, polka-dot, bikini"?'

'Easy up.' He mock-scowled before returning to his breakfast. 'I just think it'd be a challenge. The guys at the gym keep going on about how I've got great genetics for it. Thought I could give it a shot.'

Sophie lowered the mug. 'You *do* know what that entails, right? Enough bronzer to suffocate a cat and a teeny-weeny-boy- ... well, speedo.' She giggled, took another sip of her drink and choked on it. Coffee dribbled from her mouth.

Jett swallowed his last mouthful of food and pushed back his chair. Pointing his fork at her, he said, 'Serves you right.' He laughed as she coughed spasmodically while he cleaned up the pan and put his dirty dishes in the dishwasher. 'Gotta go, Soph, but I promise to give you a hand with packing tonight. Oh, and that scholarship thingy starts in a couple of weeks, right?'

'Yeah. Well, a week-and-a-half. For some reason I'm starting on a Thursday. Think it's to do with staff availability. I'll be at Advance Research Institute.'

He turned around and pinned her with his eyes. 'ARI? You seriously want to do that to yourself, after what happened with Blaine?'

Sophie shrugged, but Jett didn't miss the way her shoulders bunched. 'It'll be fine. Those people aren't there anymore, and it's the best match for my career goals.'

Silently he added what she wasn't saying, that her ultimate goal was to discover a cure for Blaine—a cure that couldn't go wrong, the way his last one had. And for all her outward calm, she couldn't hide the increased tension that had crept into her facial muscles. He knew his twin. She was stressing out over it.

'Hey, do you want me to drop you off on your first day? I can swing by on my way to our next work site in Ipswich. It's some big paying thing our boss won the tender on and it's kinda on the way.'

Sophie's face lifted and her shoulders lost their constricted angle. 'Thanks, Jett, that'd be great.'

He grabbed his lunchbox and tugged her hair as he passed. She extracted herself from the chair and trailed him to the door as he pulled on his steel-cap boots. He pretended he couldn't feel her eyes drilling through him from behind, but eventually gave in to her probing.

Without looking, he asked, 'What?'

'You know Mum's gonna see that packet in the

bin, and then you'll be G.O.N.E.'

He paused with one foot booted. 'They're not in the bin anymore.'

'Did you flush them?' She squeezed in beside him and sat on the step.

Jett chanced a glance at his sister. Her green eyes were radiating nearly as much as those stupid pills. 'I took them out this morning 'cause they were glowing enough to light up the room.'

Her face scrunched. 'Glowing?'

'Yeah. Any idea what that might be?'

She pushed to her feet, using his broad shoulder for support. 'Methinks Luca's playing a practical joke on you. It's probably fluorescein or something. You know, the same as used in eye stain tests?'

'Maybe.' Jett shrugged off the uncomfortable knowing of Luca's glowing eyes. Fluorescein stain didn't appear then disappear within seconds, nor in that colour spectrum. Standing to his full height, such that he was head and shoulders above his twin, he picked up his refreshed gym kit from where he'd put it near the front door. 'See you tonight.'

'See you, bro. And hey, you don't always have to be the easy-going nice guy. Anyone else, and you'd be calling them out. Why do you let it slide whenever Luca gives you flak? He's had a target on you to join his little focus group nearly as long as he's been gym manager. Just dob him in.'

Jett didn't answer as he headed for the car. Whatever Luca's joke, he'd have to figure it out later. *But report him?* That would mean *lots* of trouble. But maybe Sophie was right.

Chapter 3

Jett was finishing his last lunge when Imogen Gale entered the room. As if on cue, the music dropped a few decibels and the guys working out nearby stopped to stare. He felt like ten physio bands were wrapped around his chest and nearly didn't make it back up to a standing position. Setting the barbell back on the stand, he wondered if Imogen—or Gen, as she was often called—had noticed his falter. Not that it mattered. Imogen was twenty and didn't even know he existed.

He was towelling his face when he sensed her moving across the room. This week the strands of her finely braided hair were dyed a radiant fuchsia. The way she styled them made her look like a Viking warrior.

Jett forced himself to breathe—and it was nothing to do with his physical exertion. The other guys still gawked, but when one of them faked a pass at her, she effortlessly kicked his legs out from under him. She made self-defence moves look more elegant than a waltz. Jett smothered a smile as the guy landed hard on his side, and focussed on folding his towel. Imogen could look after herself.

Jett's stomach clenched when Luca followed after her and sidled up, coiling an arm around Gen's mega-toned abs, visible below her workout crop.

'How's my Muay Thai champ today?'

He contemplated offering her his towel to flick Luca off, but chewed the inside of his cheek and walked away. *Just keep it cool, Jett.* Nearly to the locker room, he heard firm footsteps behind him.

'I didn't hear a thanks, Jetto.'

Jett fisted his towel and debated whether to respond. He twisted slowly and looked Luca in the eye. 'Thanks for *what*, Luca?'

'My gift. But make sure you don't take them all at once.'

Jett raised his chin. 'All I found was rubbish someone left in my bag. Put it where it belongs.' Jett saw a threat flash through Luca's hazel eyes. He turned away, only to be reefed back around 180 degrees. Luca's hand bit into his skin as he slammed him against the wall. The weird glow brightened his eyes.

Jerking away, Jett tried dislodging Luca's hold. His arm was being crushed. 'Let me go.'

Before he could blink, Luca had him pinned against

the wall at the chest. Their noses nearly touched as the other man snorted hot, angry breaths. With his heart punching his compressed ribs, Jett stared into the manager's reddened face. His eyes were blazing the fluorescent green with rippling rainbow hues that was becoming frighteningly familiar.

'Seriously, dude, what's up with you?' Jett gasped, feeling like his chest might cave.

Luca leaned in, the force of his hand like a parked truck. 'You need to learn a little gratitude, *Jetto*.' His face contorted, as if he were in pain.

Jett shuddered as Luca bared his teeth, which were also glowing. *What the—?* Next thing he was pushed up the wall until his feet dangled. His pulse pounded like a sub-woofer in his ears—da-doef, da-doef.

'I. Am. Fine.' Luca's voice was nearly an octave deeper than usual.

Black teased Jett's vision like threads of a raw hem when a voice called out.

'Luca, what are you doing?' Gen's words pitched up in alarm as she approached them from the main corridor.

Jett wondered if she could see the way Luca's muscles bulged like a superhero caricature, and the green-to-rainbow flashes highlighting his veins.

'Let the kid be.'

The kid? Now he wasn't only invisible, he was juvenile.

Instantly the pressure of Luca's arm released and Jett dropped to the floor. He landed hard on flat feet and sucked in lungsful of air.

'I was just helping Jetto here with some stretches, babe.' Luca arranged his face into a half-smile and patted Jett on the shoulder.

'Yeah, really looked like it.'

Jett palmed Luca away and backed shakily into the locker room. He grabbed his gym bag and hurried to the exit. A thousand retorts marched through his mind. He should have said more; should have made it clear to Luca he'd never stoop that low. With agitated moves and a mental apology to Sophie for stinking up the car, he escaped to the vehicle and left.

So reporting you, dude.

Jett's hands were still trembling as he retreated to his bedroom and closed the door. He'd been halfway home before his teeth had stopped chattering, never mind his ribs feeling like they might be detached from his sternum. He didn't want to ring the police, but Luca had totally tripped his wire. This was *way* above the gym owners' jurisdiction.

He searched up the crime stoppers number and went to his desk to get the glow-in-the-dark pills, but his attention was drawn to a small brown gift bag on the top of his desk. *Okay?*

Pressing away folds of tissue paper, he extracted a gold, sequined G-string. 'Sophie!' His body ignited at the thought of wearing it. Maybe he *wasn't* up for that comp after all. Shaking his head, he opened the drawer where he'd stored the pills. It was empty. Pressure mushroomed inside him.

'Jett?' His mum's voice breached the stunned pause. Milliseconds later the door of his room opened.

Jett turned to face her, the glittering G-string still hanging from his finger. 'Mum, where's my stuff?'

Her cheeks bloomed red as her eyes found the flashy underwear. 'I ... ah ... what's with the glammed-up jocks? Do I even *want* to know?'

Dropping the 'gift' back in the bag, Jett couldn't shutdown the fire burning his face. *Man, it's hot in here.* 'Probably not. But when Soph gets home, I'm gonna have words.'

'Okay ...'

'The stuff from my desk?'

'I was on a roll. I'm back to work next week, so ...' Her face filled with concern and her gaze drifted again to the gift bag. 'Jett, may I ask you something?'

Jett knew that look anywhere. 'You found the pills.' He sighed. There was no point beating around the bush.

Her brow lined, each crease underscoring her worry. She extended her hand and unfurled her fingers, revealing the small packet of pills on her palm. 'Can you help me understand why you had them in your drawer?'

'It was a stupid prank by the gym manager. He's being a jerk. Acting ... freaky.'

'Freaky?'

'It doesn't matter, I just ...' He took the pills from his mother and shrugged. 'I'll get rid of them, okay? Don't even know what they are.'

'Alright honey. I know you'll do the right thing.' She patted his arm. 'You're okay though?'

Was he? Jett gave another half-hearted shrug. It was time to call the cops.

Chapter 4

The gym was a lather of activity next time Jett went in. He wasn't sure what would cause more suspicion—ending his membership immediately and changing gyms, or going along as if he had no idea someone had tipped off the police. He wasn't sure when they'd undertake their investigation, only that they would.

Deciding to keep his usual routine—as if there wasn't a mini-blizzard going on in his chest cavity, cold and swirling—Jett turned up at his usual time and dropped his kit in a locker. As he passed the bodybuilding comp poster, his steps slowed like a remote-control car with the battery running low. *Could I?*

Last night Sophie had done some research on non-steroid means of bulking swiftly and, in discussion with some of his workout buddies, had helped him put together a routine that might get him over the line. He studied the poster a moment longer before continuing to the workout room.

When he'd finished his session, Jett headed for

the showers. Two men awaited him. They were in plain clothes, but had badges. Tasers. Guns. Cuffs.

'Jett Faraday?'

'Yeah?' Despite a sheen of sweat on his skin, the iciness in his chest intensified. *Shouldn't they be, like, questioning Luca?*

'I'm Senior Constable Gassmann.' He flashed a badge, then introduced his partner. 'We'd like to ask you a few questions.'

'You guys … um … know—' He glanced around to ensure they were alone. '—I was the one who made the call?'

'And we're following up, like we said. Do you mind if we take a look in your locker?'

'Sure.' Yet Jett was anything but sure. There was something about their tone that made him feel like he'd pushed himself too hard on the bench and couldn't get the bar back on the stand. As he dialled in the locker code, the mini-blizzard inside spread like a snap freeze through his body.

He waited as they pulled on gloves; lifted out his kit; searched the locker. Nothing. Then they started on the contents of his bag. He began shivering as his spare shirt, shorts, underwear and toiletries were laid out on the locker-room bench.

'You seem nervous, Jett. Any reason you might be worried?'

He shook his head and tried to stop shaking. 'Nah.'

'The gym manager said you've been making some pretty impressive gains lately,' Gassmann shared as he burrowed into the side pocket of Jett's kit. He pulled out two packs of pills and a registration form for the bodybuilding comp.

The freeze hit Jett's heart and for a second he was sure it stopped beating. These weren't glow-in-the-dark capsules, but straight-out steroids. Or worse. He tried to swallow, but his throat stuck to itself like clingwrap. So, it wasn't just going to be intimidation. Luca was out for revenge.

'Care to explain?'

'I can't. They're not mine.'

'It's your kit though, isn't it? You packed it? It's been in a secure locker since you got here, correct?'

'Yeah.'

'Anyone else have access?'

'The manager.'

'He's been with us the whole time you've been here.'

So, they'd been waiting for him.

'We're going to do a quick test. Take this, wipe it down your tongue a couple of times.'

Jett did as he was told and handed back the plastic tongue scraper. They then supplied a urine jar, which he was required to fill in front of them. It felt like he was trapped in a sauna. Waves of heat rolled over his body, enveloping his skin and melting the cold that had moments earlier paralysed him. 'The test'll come back negative. I don't do drugs. Or steroids. I've been set-up.' By Luca. *Jerk.*

'That's for us to decide.' Gassmann undertook some rapid tests and checked the results. They were negative for illicit substances. 'This doesn't mean you're off the hook. These are going for full lab analysis.' He passed the samples to his partner then turned his attention to the pills.

'They're not mine. You can print check them. Use DNA—whatever. I'm guessing it's a warning because I asked you to investigate.'

'That's your version of events. The manager says he called *you* out on this, which made you panic—hence your call to us to cover your trail. And now we've found this.' He held up the pack of pills, which a quick test determined to be methamphetamine. The other was likely testosterone.

'Luca's lying. I said they're not mine.'

Gassmann handed the evidence to his partner and ignored this claim. 'Jett, you've got no record to date. Given this is a first offence, we're only going to fine you for possession of a restricted substance. In the meantime, how about you take a break from the gym and make some smarter choices. We catch you back here with anything like this, and you'll be answering to a magistrate.'

Jett said nothing as they handed him the fine. Teeth clenched hard enough to crack, he waited until they were gone before shoving the displaced contents of his kit back in the bag. He got the message loud and clear. Either shut up or be shut up. But this wasn't over by a long shot. No way was he going to let this one slide. He just had to figure out his next move.

'Check this, Soph.' Jett barged into his twin's bedroom and slapped the fine on the desk in front of her.

There was a slight pause as Sophie read the document. She then swivelled on her office chair and searched him. 'Seriously?' Her rounded eyes lit with confusion.

Jett slumped into a beanbag near her, his prior

resolve as shapeless as the beans now squashed under him. He dropped his head onto his palms. 'Somehow he set me up while I was doing my workout.'

'Don't go anymore. He's clearly got a problem and isn't afraid to drag you down with him.'

'Understatement of the decade,' he muttered, saving her the details of Luca's weird glow-in-the-dark features. It just didn't make sense. The dude was clearly doing more than steroids. Fact was, it seemed to give him superpowers. How strong did he need to be before he was satisfied? But what was it and where was Luca getting it?

He lifted his head out of his palms as a plan flickered in his mind. That was the first thing he had to find out—the source of the pills. Dragging himself up, he said, 'Better go de-stink. Sorry to interrupt. And don't tell Mum. She'll flip.'

'Jett, she's a clinical engineer, not a PI, but she'll work it out. She's Mum.'

Sophie's ominous warning tracked him out the door. She was right, of course. Just because their mum was in a buzz about getting everything moved before her brief leave ended didn't mean she wasn't overtly aware of everything that happened in their home. Before that occurred, he had to find out more about those capsules.

Chapter 5

Jett lowered the binoculars and pressed his head back against the car-seat headrest. *Three a.m.* He yawned. The problem with 24-hour gyms was they never closed. He could be here until dawn.

Having borrowed his parents' car to minimise the chance of Luca spotting and identifying the vehicle, he was now positioned across the road from the gym carpark. Thus far, he'd not seen the manager enter or leave. This made him wonder if Luca had gone home after the police raid. *Unlikely.*

Cars came and went with no sign of Luca. Jett glanced at the dash clock. It was now nearly four o'clock. With a groan he realised he had to leave for work in an hour and a half. His mum would also be champing at the bit if he didn't have the car back for her next early moving frenzy. Surely with Luca's intense workout schedule he hadn't gone over twenty-four hours without sleep?

Tempted to sneak in, he knew the building access points were under video surveillance. *If only I could get into Luca's office without being seen.*

Another ten minutes passed and his time was up. Finger on the engine start button, he caught sight of a deep blue sedan pulling up in the empty gym park. Interestingly, the driver didn't get out of the car. Easing his hand away from the starter, he watched as Luca emerged from the building.

If the guy hadn't slept in a day, there was no evidence. In fact, he looked like he'd just finished a workout. Muscles carved his body, yet there didn't seem to be the slightest hint of sweat slicking his hair or skin as he swaggered across the carpark.

Jett held his breath, hoping Luca wouldn't turn around and notice his car, or him. There was a brief exchange between the gym manager and the driver of the other vehicle. Then, a palm-sized black packet was passed to Luca through the window. *The capsules.* It was either that or a delivery of steroids, which he knew Luca was supplying to some of the gym members. Either way, it was his best hunch after a long night.

Waiting until the car was leaving, Jett pressed the start button and shifted the gearstick to drive. Once Luca was back in the building, he pulled out and followed the car.

In the sparse, early morning traffic, it was easy to

keep the blue vehicle in sight. What was more difficult was keeping far enough back to not draw suspicion from the driver. *Are they on alert? Did they notice me pull out? Is there a second person in the passenger seat?* He wasn't sure, but he might have seen another head.

After following the car for nearly twenty minutes he drew back further, only to have a tow truck pull out of a side street, between him and the car. *Man!* He didn't want to tailgate but he couldn't see around the cumbersome vehicle in front. Speeding up, he edged nearer the centre of the street to try and catch a glimpse of the vehicle two ahead. It was gone.

Jett batted the steering wheel with his palm. Easing his foot off the accelerator, he let the distance between his car and the truck widen. He then indicated for the next side street on the left to initiate a U-turn.

As he swung around one-eighty in the side street, he caught a glimpse of the deep blue car halfway along it. Heartrate crunching up a gear, he braked and stared in his rear-view mirror as the blue car pulled up outside a drab-looking brown brick building in the street behind him. *Do I turn around again?* He couldn't sit at the intersection with right-hand indicator flashing forever.

Deciding a drive by would be the least intrusive mode of surveillance, he checked the clock. He had to get moving if he was to get to work on time. Grateful it was too early for the morning traffic rush, he U-turned again on the main road, back into the side street.

Jett maintained a speed that was slow enough to take a good look, but not so steady it would draw excess attention. Ahead, the driver's door opened and a man got out. Glancing about, the man took a passing look at the approaching vehicle Jett was driving, but gave no hint of recognition. As he closed the door and walked around the car to the kerb, the passenger door swung open.

Huh? Jett hadn't been imagining a second person. Keeping his face forward as if oblivious to the parked sedan, he checked his left-hand side mirror as he drove beyond, allowing him to sight the passenger exiting the car. The first thing he registered was the flaming braids coiled into a messy bun atop their head.

It was Gen.

Jett's head swam like a school of fish. Once she came into sight in his rear-view mirror he stared at her shrinking profile until he nearly didn't stop at the T-intersection at the far end of the street.

Did she see me? What's her involvement? Why did she stop Luca attacking me if she knows what's going on?

It made no sense. What he *did* know was he had to get home fast, or he'd get his butt kicked by his boss.

Either way, he'd be back to investigate soon, even if it meant another all-night stake-out.

Chapter 6

'Where are you off to? You only just got home from work.' Sophie stood in the doorway of her bedroom as Jett emerged from his room with gym kit in hand.

'Where's it look like I'm going?' he said, sounding more uptight than a rowing machine set to highest resistance.

His twin slouched against the door jamb and folded her arms, sending a squirm through his insides. 'See, you might *say* you're the brawns and I'm the brains, but you're not an idiot. And only someone with *zero* intelligence would be heading back there after what happened yesterday.'

Jett gave an offhanded shrug as his eyes strayed to the nearby landing, marking his escape route.

'Mum said she left you a note about helping Dad pull down beds and desks after work, before the removalists come tomorrow morning.'

He shrugged again. 'Yeah, got it.'

'Well, that would be *now*, Jett. Dad's already

working on Anna's bedroom. Mine's next.'

Jett blew out a breath and placed his gym kit back inside his room, next to the door. He'd have to follow-up on the brown brick building later. Maybe it was a good thing, given how sleep deprived he was from his all-night adventure. 'Fine. Where's the toolbox?'

Sophie pursed her lips to the side. 'Not saying until you tell me where you went last night.'

Man! No doubt Sophie had been reading up on something late when he'd snuck out—and semester wasn't even in. 'Mum knows I borrowed the car.'

'I *know* that. I want to know *where* you went.'

With a small shake of his head, Jett bypassed her and retreated to Anna's room to help their dad. No way was he putting his twin or any family member in the middle of this.

Despite his investigative ambitions, over a week passed before Jett was able to escape the work-clean-unpack cycle. Mum was back at work, Anna had one more week of school for the year, and Dad had lost some of his moving-related stress habits.

He had to admit that even though the new house wasn't far from their old one, the views of Moreton Bay from their front yard and deck made moving worth the effort. The house had a pretty sweet holiday vibe. *Need to have Blaine over for a housewarming visit.* He'd also found a new gym five minutes away by car and, with his new regime, was bulking faster than ever. Satisfied he was on track, he'd registered for the body building competition.

All thoughts of holiday vibes and muscle gain fled his mind as he leaned back in the car seat and watched the brown brick building across the street. He'd arrived shortly after midnight. Now, several hours later, the building remained as still as the night air. Despite it being the first week of summer, he'd dressed in a black, long sleeve, dry-fit shirt and a pair of long black cargo pants. He figured a black beanie might be pushing it, so he'd added a black cap instead—anything to make him less visible.

Learning from his last sneak out, Jett had checked Sophie's bedroom light was off before walking quietly to front door. *Flip, she stayed up late.* He'd been tempted to borrow Dad's car, but hadn't wanted to create a fuss. Besides, his and Sophie's shared vehicle was parked under the carport, rather than garaged. Opening the garage would have certainly risked waking people. If he'd been caught at such an odd hour, he would have spent until dawn being grilled by his parents and twin.

Now he just had to wait.

And wait.

And wait.

Another hour dripped by and the sky lightened with the approach of dawn. Scanning again for surveillance cameras, he'd not seen any evidence of security, but knew that didn't mean it wasn't there. Could he do a quick scout around the property?

He glanced at the clock as the sky brightened further. If he didn't go now, it would be fully daylight— then he'd have no cover at all.

Ensuring the interior car lights were off, he touched the door lever ready to open it. The approach of a flat-bed delivery truck made him pause. Sweat broke over him as the truck stopped alongside his car. What if it was bringing supplies to the building and being offloaded roadside? What if someone came out and saw him parked there? What if— He then heard the driver shift the vehicle into reverse and blew out a breath.

As it backed into the driveway of the building across from him, a light went on at the side of the property. *Sensor light?* Either that, or the place was attended, even at this hour.

Before leaving the car, he waited for the driver to

get out and start offloading things at the rear of the truck. If someone was lurking about, the place he'd parked meant the truck would block the view of his car from the building. He walked down the driver's side, between the truck and a fence built of the same tired, brown brick as the two-story structure.

Light shone between the tyres. He squatted down to peer through the gap, using the rear tyres as a barrier. It was a bit early for a courier service.

Someone was being asked their name for signing the delivery docket. Ivan Novik. Why did that name sound so familiar? He squirrelled it away for later as he peered between the wheelbase at Ivan's shoes, visible on the elevated loading dock.

Ivan retreated and another person came out and started shifting the stock inside. A smouldering cigarette butt landed on the ground below the dock and smoke drifted to where Jett was waiting. He blew out air, as if this could dilute the acrid particles invading his nostrils. The driver went to the back for more goods and Jett saw his chance. He crawled under the truck, then pulled himself up onto the raised platform. The door into the building was open.

He grabbed a twenty-litre drum filled with liquid and carried it inside. Following the lingering scent of tobacco smoke, he was led to a service lift. Ensuring the person ahead was busy depositing their load, he placed the drum near them. Before they noticed him, he ducked behind a stack of boxes at the side of the room.

Watching, he noted the level to which goods were sent—basement—and searched about the room with his eyes for a way to gain access. Stairs? Elevator? He couldn't see anything obvious.

The person—a woman, as he could now see— turned around and nearly fell over the drum he'd left behind her. She frowned, shrugged and added it to the goods she'd already placed in the lift. '*Thanks*, Ivan.'

Closing the door of the service lift, she pressed the button again to deliver the second load. She then crossed the room perilously close to where Jett was hiding and disappeared through a gap between walls he'd missed.

Following, Jett heard a door clunk shut. He peered around the wall, into a stairwell that descended to a lower floor in the building. The basement. Checking no one was else was nearby, he eased down the stairs on silent feet.

Light shone through a viewing pane in a door at the bottom of the stairs. Approaching it, he heard voices. Both were familiar, but he immediately recognised one.

Gen.

Edging up to the door, he looked through the glass into a … *production room?* There were vats and tubes, chemicals and automated capsule fillers, and instruments he didn't recognise. In the middle of this space Gen faced Ivan. Braids, now cyan blue—she liked to keep her look fresh—were pulled into a loose ponytail. Her voice was raised and her index finger was making swift jabs in the man's direction.

The mental gears clicked and Jett realised why Ivan seemed familiar. He was a casual PT at his gym—correction, his old gym—who usually went by the name 'Van'. The guy had some Eastern European-type accent and impressive credentials that allowed him to consult on training regimes for personnel from police departments to the highest level of government forces. It had always seemed strange to Jett that Ivan had bothered with such an ordinary job as a PT in a small, local gym. Interestingly, Ivan had started with the gym not long after Luca had taken over as manager.

Easing his mobile phone from his pocket, Jett snapped off a few pictures of the room, whilst eavesdropping on the exchange.

'You said it wouldn't be detrimental.'

Ivan raised his hands, as if that could fend off an

enraged Gen. Although, of all the people Jett knew, Ivan was the one who might stand a chance against her in a fight.

'Imogen, you are upset for nothing. He is responding exactly as we expect.'

'You call this a *performance* enhancer? What's with the fluorescing crap?' She looked like she might dismember him with her bare hands. 'He's more volatile than an unstable nuclear reactor.'

'The term is performance modification, and it's only natural some of his responses will be unpredictable until we gain a handle on him.'

'You mean *crazy*. And the glow?'

Ivan shrugged. 'The glow is merely an internal validation ... proof-of-concept ... ensuring the correct incorporation of the technology into the body. It should not be required for post-trial applications.'

'You need to stop him taking it.'

Ivan laughed ominously. 'Once he has taken three doses there is no not taking it. The modifications are irreversible.'

Gen's mouth fell open. Jett gulped.

'What does *that* mean?'

'Three doses and it reaches saturation in the system. More merely intensifies the indomitability of the consumer, but the construct swiftly finds its place. Permanently.'

Three doses. That's what Luca had left in his gym bag. But what was this construct Ivan was talking about? It certainly wasn't a building.

'So … nothing can stop his aggressive … overreactions?' Gen's arms sank to her sides as if she had been pinned down by invisible restraints.

'There is a neutralising antidote that can temporarily block the mechanism, but the genetically encoded proteins rapidly express and remain in place. Further supplementation retriggers the effects.' As if to prove this, he unlocked a drawer near them and pulled out an unusual looking autoinjector. Gen's eyes latched on the preloaded drug injector. 'But there is no reason to block. He is invincible. Just as we intended. And when the time is right, we will demonstrate that his strength and fearlessness can be controlled and will prove useful.'

'Controlled? How?' A look of fear twisted Gen's face and Jett's chest tightened. Was she safe with Ivan? The guy was ridiculously muscular and, by the sounds of it, not exactly sane. Why was Ivan wanting to make Luca crazy *and* invincible?

Gotta get in there and snoop around.

Ivan placed the autoinjector on the bench above

the drawer and turned away. Gen hesitated as he strode across the production area, out a door on the opposite side. Tracking the man with her eyes, she swiped the injector, pocketed it, and followed.

Once they'd left, Jett tested the door handle and discovered it unlocked. He stepped silently into the room and scanned the equipment at the front. His eyes swept to the far wall at the back of the space. A strange chemical smell with a hint of tobacco smoke hung in the air. There was a whiteboard off to one side with diagrams and chemical formulas scribbled across it. Goosebumps dimpled his skin as he surveyed the information.

Glancing at the doors on either side of the room, he ensured the coast was still clear before approaching the whiteboard. It was a flow diagram, but it seemed incomplete. Reaching back to high school biology, he recognised a cell membrane as part of what looked like a roughly drawn nerve cell. Through the membrane layers was sketched a hollow, oblong shape. *Protein?*

An arrow pointed from another structure with several chemical formulas attached, towards the shape he thought could be a membrane protein. A second arrow drew his eye to another structure with another nerve-looking cell attached to a DNA-like drawing and an additional chemical formula. Written at the top of this section of the board was 'modified magneto'. The words 'fluorescent signal' were written alongside this and on the opposite side, was a number with 'MHz' written next to it. Megahertz? Frequency?

It was moments like now he wished he had Sophie's smarts. Somehow, he'd have to figure it out. Taking photos of the diagram and formulas, and then the room, he pocketed the phone and checked the area again for additional information. Deciding he'd seen enough, Jett moved towards the door through which he'd entered.

Pulling on the handle, he heard a soft click across the room. Blood bulleted through his arteries and his head whooshed as he swung the door open and slipped into the stairwell. Without warning, his phone sprang to life. *No way!* He'd forgot to set it on silent.

Focus snapping back through the viewing glass, he saw Gen in full view with Ivan close behind. Her eyes locked onto his as he snatched the phone from his pocket and turned off the ringer. Fleeing up the steps two at a time, he saw Sophie's name illuminated on the screen.

Scrambling around the corner at the top of the steps, he nearly collided with the woman who'd been relocating stock. How? It proved there must be another exit from the basement.

'Who are *you*?' she said as Jett shouldered her away.

Sprinting for the exit, he still couldn't figure out why Sophie was calling him so early. Why was she awake at all, given her aversion to mornings? Jostling the key remote from his pocket as he ran, he unlocked the car, ran to the driver's door and yanked it open. Dropping into the seat, he slammed the door shut.

Fingers fumbling, it took three attempts to get the key in the ignition, before turning over the engine. Glancing out the passenger's window, he dropped the clutch as the rising sun lit up Gen and Ivan's silhouettes crossing the street. In the milliseconds it took the car to lurch forward with wheels spinning, they reached the space where Jett had been parked. Ivan's hand slapped the back corner of the hatch as the car sped off.

Chapter 7

Jett pulled up in the driveway at home and flattened his back against the seat. An accident has caused a bottleneck partway home, so it had taken the best part of an hour to get back. Now, traffic was horrible.

Still, his heart drummed at his throat and his hands shook from the intense hit of adrenaline. He didn't want to think about what Gen and Ivan might do or say to Luca. Taking a few breaths to steady himself, he finally went inside.

The house was quieter than he'd expected for six-thirty in the morning. *Six-thirty?* How did it get so late? Today his trade group were starting that big job in Ipswich. He needed to be gone forty minutes ago, on a *good* commute day.

Striding along the hall to his room, he pushed open the door and came face-to-face with his twin. She was sitting on his bed and wearing a nice pair of pants and a business-like shirt. Her curly hair was pulled back in a ponytail and her eyes cut him like a chef knife.

'A – Where have you been? And B – What's today, Jett?'

A billow of steam out of her ears would have been an appropriate visual for her tone.

Ignoring her, he ripped the black, long-sleeved shirt over his head and exchanged it for a high-visibility shirt from his wardrobe. He could feel her glaring at him and wished she'd drop the cryptic rubbish. But then the date cannonballed his stomach like a fast thrown kettlebell.

He spun around. 'Soph, your first day with ARI. I'm sorry. I forgot.'

'Yeah, well, now I'm going to be *totally* late! I'm supposed to be there *early* so I can finalise some paperwork and inductions before I start at *eight*.'

'Why didn't you take the train?'

'And a bus, and another bus. *Could* have, *if* you hadn't pre-arranged to drop me off on the way to your worksite in Ipswich.' Her voice rose with each word. 'Where have you been?'

'Give me a sec to change my pants, Soph, and we'll go. This is my bad. I'll call your supervisor *and* my boss on the way and wear it.'

She didn't argue as she left the room, but her shoulders remained unnaturally squared. He mentally calculated how long it would take to get to the opposite quadrant of Brisbane from Moreton Bay, *before* continuing to his worksite, in what was turning into crazier-than-usual morning traffic. Dragging on his work boots and grabbing the lunchbox he'd prepared the night before, Jett's stomach howled with hunger. There would be no breakfast cook up today.

Back at the car, Sophie was in the driver's seat, car idling. She'd left the front passenger door open in readiness for him. His sister was reversing before he'd fully shut the door. 'Easy, you'll swipe the door off on the gate.' She said nothing as she shifted gears and zoomed away. The set of her jaw told him she was still fuming.

He held onto the roof handle as she barely slowed to take a round-about. The radio was off, and she'd not turned on her usual playlist or even bluetoothed one from her phone.

'You know, it'd help if we got there alive, madzilla.'

'I'm not mad,' Sophie snapped, face turned away as she checked for oncoming traffic to the right.

'Sure seems like it.' He rolled his eyes and tightened his grip on the overhead support. He'd be relieved when they hit the motorway.

'Where were you?' This time her voice broke,

spearing him with guilt.

'Soph, you don't need to be worried.'

'I *am* worried. You were dressed like a burglar. This is something like Blaine would do.' She caught his eye for an instant. 'You're the sensible one, not the impulsive one with a death wish.'

He heard her gasp as soon as she said the words. They both knew Blaine's death could be a reality if anything changed with his health, not that anyone really talked about it much. He wondered what else had Sophie so worked up. 'This isn't only about me, is it?'

She didn't answer as she accelerated and merged onto the motorway. Despite the rough drive, they were making such good time, she was likely to get to ARI earlier than she needed. Typical Sophie. Always stressing that she wouldn't exceed expectations. Simply meeting them was never enough for her.

'Soph, you don't need to worry about me. I'm big an' ugly enough to look after myself, okay?'

She snorted. 'Ugly? Better tell that to all the girls who fliff and preen wherever you go.'

'That's just 'cause I can lift heavy things.' He was relieved when a small smile crinkled the corner of her mouth.

'So can Luca, but the guy's a creep.'

Something about her tone rang an alarm in him. 'What's Luca got to do with anything?'

She changed lanes then answered. 'He baled me up last night during my shift at the restaurant. Came in. Made a scene. Kept asking where you work out now; claimed you weren't man enough to take up his challenge.' Catching his eye for a second, she admitted, 'He really scared me, Jett. He was out of control. And there was something freaky happening with his eyes.'

Jett felt like someone had thrown up on him. His own stomach started churning to the point it hurt. No way was Luca threatening his sister and getting away with it. No. Flipping. Way. 'I'll go see him after work.'

Sophie's whole body coiled towards him, sending the car lurching to the edge of the lane and back.

'Easy, Soph.'

'No, Jett, leave it please. My boss reported him to the police and they've made a note of the incident. You don't have to take all the hits for me. Like now, you're going to cop it from your boss *and* cover for me—though technically this *is* your fault.'

'You don't understand, Soph, Luca's ... enhanced.' It was lame, but the best he could do without spilling his covert outings to his twin.

'Enhanced?' Her neatly groomed eyebrows

arched.

'I can't explain it any better, but I think it's to do with those pills.'

'Well, I hope his brain decomposes,' she muttered in an unusual show of venom.

Though he rarely admitted it, Sophie was a total sweetheart. If Luca had scared her enough to draw insults like that, nothing was stopping him from putting the chemically-induced maniac in his place. 'Did you tell Blaine about it?' He knew if his mate heard about Luca threatening Sophie, he'd be there with a baseball bat to back him up.

Sophie's mouth drooped, like she was about to cry. 'I couldn't get onto him,' she admitted, her voice raspy.

Right. Sophie was scared *and* missing her nearly boyfriend. 'It's probably best you don't tell Blaine about Luca. He'd only put himself in the line of fire, and you know Blaine won't back down.'

She nodded. 'True, and I know I said you don't always have to be the easy-going nice guy, but I still think *you* shouldn't confront him either.'

He shrugged. 'I'll see how the day goes.'

They fell silent and he decided to google some of the information he'd photographed in the production room. First, the mysterious 'modified magneto'. After trowelling through pages of X-Men hits, he found an article that piqued his interest. Clicking the link, he read the information.

It turned out 'magneto' was a biological device … *device? … protein maybe?* … enabling remote control—*like how?*—of neural circuits associated with complex animal behaviours. That must have been what Ivan meant when he said they could control Luca. From this, it wasn't clear how that control could be exerted.

Next, he googled some of the chemical formulas. One proved particularly interesting. It was a metallic oxide that was superparamagnetic in biological systems. A magneto-like protein and a superparamagnetic compound? By the diagram they seemed to be linked somehow. *And what's this?*

Clicking on another search result, he read about how attaching genetically engineered nerve cell proteins to paramagnetic particles could make them sensitive to radio waves and magnetic fields. Radio waves? Could Luca be remote controlled?

Maybe it was more complicated than it sounded. And the DNA-looking sequence? Could they be telling the body to make those proteins? *If only I could ask Sophie.*

'What are you looking at?' Sophie's question

came on cue, as if he'd spoken aloud. She glanced at the phone screen.

Jett automatically angled the phone away and didn't miss his sister's frown. He'd heard of twins having unusual connections. Maybe this applied to them, given his last thought. 'Just trying to figure something out.'

'Now you're starting to *act* like Blaine.' She shot him a pointed glance.

Grinning, Jett said, 'Yeah, but I know you think he's a pretty okay kinda guy.' In a fluid move, her fist bumped his shoulder. 'Ow. Keep your hands on the wheel.'

'I didn't hit you hard.' Though Sophie's expression was smug.

Rolling his eyes, Jett hunted for additional details.

He figured he had about ten minutes until they reached ARI. Switching to Google Scholar, he did a little more searching and found some of the other formulations were associated with technology called optogenetics. This also seemed to focus on controlling specific neural pathways, but using light to turn key protein pathways on and off. The fluorescence? But didn't Ivan say that was mainly a check of the system? The other compound brought up a link to nanoparticles associated with delivering constructs for gene therapy.

The DNA. Whoa, maybe *that's* what Ivan meant.

It seemed they were either trying to work out the most effective approach, meaning Luca was a human guinea pig, or there were multiple systems in play. What that ultimately meant was certainly beyond his pay grade.

Glancing up, he saw the entrance to ARI ahead. 'Are you nervous?'

A tense smile thinned Sophie's mouth. 'Yeah, a bit.'

'Well, I know you'll smash it.' He nudged her with his elbow. 'And how 'bout I give Blaine a call later to arrange a catch up? It's been over a month since we've done a workout together. Once you've settled into your summer scholarship lab thing, we could do a night out?'

Her smiled broadened as they pulled into the driveway of ARI. Still, she seemed to be masking uncertainty. 'That'd be nice. And don't forget Dad's taking me home this afternoon.'

'Yeah, yeah. Sorry. I don't usually forget. I've just had a lot on my mind.' He caught her arm as she stopped in a five minute drop off point. 'Soph, it'll be okay.'

She nodded as if convincing herself and patted his shoulder. 'See you later, fit boy.'

He smiled to reassure her as he got out to take

her place at the wheel, then used his adjustment of the seat for maximum leg room to hide the chaos of doubt inside him. Nothing was certain where Luca was concerned and, no matter what he told himself, his chat with the gym manager would be anything but uneventful.

Chapter 8

As Jett entered his former gym, a roar shook him with an intensity that rivalled the splintering thunderstorm booming overhead. The door closed on the fierce weather outside, but a follow-up bellow echoed from the weight area, like the cry of an enraged animal caught in a trap. The sound yielded sandpaper-like goosebumps over his body, even as heavy rain exploded on the roof above.

Resisting the urge to run, he quickened his pace past the abandoned reception desk. As the glass walls of the workout room came into view, he stopped short.

A couple of guys he used to train with were backing away from Luca. The manager was tearing—*tearing!*—apart a 20 kilo weight with his bare hands, like it was a warm chocolate button. His muscles bulged three times their normal size and glowed primarily green with rainbow pulses, making him an eerie shadow of an Incredible Hulk caricature. Strength dribbled from Jett's body as Luca bragged to the pair, telling them they could have the same type of power. All they had to do was let him know and he'd fix them up.

It was like he was recruiting for a war.

The man seemed out of his mind. *Maybe I should warn those guys?* But he knew there was nothing he could do to help them without getting pulverised by Luca.

He had to rethink his plan. No wonder Sophie had been afraid. Reason fled as another wave of anger washed through him at the thought of Luca threatening his sister.

Striding forward, something hard drove into him from aside, shunting him face first to the floor. Grunting from the heavy contact, he tried pushing himself up, but someone gripped his arms and twisted them tight behind him. Face down, he was dragged along the smooth wooden floor of the corridor, through a door, into a darkened equipment storage room. It felt like his arms were about to pop from his shoulder sockets. The door slammed shut, muffling the sound of the pummelling rain, and plunging him into blackness.

'Don't move. *Don't* speak.'

Gen? What was going on with her voice?

He flipped onto his feet in a low crouch, ready to defend himself. If she'd taken him out alone, she was stronger than he'd thought. Granted, he'd been caught off guard, but that was impressive. Fear swiftly crushed his admiration as a shimmer of green with interjecting rainbow spectrums lit her form. The same hue highlighted her eyes, matching that of Luca. Gen was neck deep in all of it.

'Why are you doing this, Imogen?'

'I could ask *you* the same thing. I said *don't* speak.'

'You've taken the pills. I can see you glowing.'

'Not exactly by choice—but that's none of your business.'

Next thing he knew, the blade of her hand chopped the side of his neck, landing him in a world of pain. Seeing stars, he felt himself being moved again and tried to fight back. He couldn't get himself together. Another door opened and a shove in the back thrust him onto a wet cement path outside the building. Landing in a crawling position under the easing rain, with grazed knees and palms, he blinked against the hint of dusk shrouded by the dense cloud cover.

'Get going and keep your nose out of it. You can thank me later.' Gen slammed the door behind him.

'Ergh.' Ignoring the water soaking into his clothes, Jett propped himself up on his side and rubbed his throbbing neck. He knew the impact pressure point move; had seen her use it to disable opponents larger than him. She could drop a guy on his face in less than a second. Shame seared him when he realised how his confrontation with Luca would have played out. She was right. He should thank her later. As for staying out of it, not in a million years.

Instead of driving home, Jett went back to the brown brick building. By the time he got there, the thunderstorm had passed and steam rose off the road, captured in eerie snapshots by the headlights of passing cars. He had to find out what they were doing and why. Luca was trying to get other guys to take the pills and was clearly frustrated by their lack of enthusiasm. Who would have thought craziness was not the best motivational strategy? *Pfft, typically clueless Luca.*

Parking in a nearby side street, he walked in darkness to the drab-looking building housing the production facility. Ensuring his phone was on silent— *learning robot*—he scouted around, front then side, hunting for an alternative way in. He tested the doors first, then the windows. Nada. Still, he didn't see any obvious security.

On the opposite side of the building to the loading dock, there were steps down to an emergency exit door at basement level. That had to be how the smoker lady got out that morning. Searching again for security cameras and finding none, he decided to try his luck.

Taking the steps as silently as he could in his work boots, he combed the door for a handle, but there wasn't one on the outside. One way access. Puffing out a breath, he was about to retreat when he heard voices on the other side of the door. He leaned his ear against the wood to listen.

'Luca is failing to sell our mission,' a man's voice said, at which someone chuckled.

'He is our experiment, no? Impressive strength but too hot-headed to handle the modulations the formula brings.' This sounded like Ivan.

'So much for raising an army,' the first man lamented. 'And we are running out of time.'

There's that army-war thing again.

'We do not need many for our test. You know the one I want. The "virtuous" one.' Ivan gave a hard laugh. 'And once we've proven ourselves capable, we can expand our reach—voluntarily or not.'

'Any news on our intruder?'

They're talking about me.

'Gen will sort it out.' Ivan's response was alarmingly

confident.

'She is modulated?'

'Not fully. Luca is putting her off, but has managed to administer two doses.'

Jett remembered Gen's 'not by choice' claim. *If Luca's forcing her to take them, why does she stick around?*

'Just one more, and she would have been fully modulated.' The second man sighed. 'No mind. She is a smaller build so this may enable enough control for our test, and assimilation is accelerated with each dose.'

A sighing creak at the rear of the building set Jett's heart pounding. Cigarette smoke drifted to where he was standing. Creeping away from the door, he knew he had to get inside. Hugging the building wall, he followed the smoke to the corner.

Peering around the back, he saw an unkempt carpark filling the space between the building and a brick fence at the property's rear boundary. The woman who had been helping offload goods that morning was sitting on a retaining wall a metre from the back door. Her cigarette glowed orange each time she drew on it. As if agitated, she was flicking the roller on a cigarette lighter, making the flame flare over and again. He jumped as the back door banged open.

'I've told you not to do that near the doors *or* inside—and don't tell me it's not you. The smoke's drifting all the way downstairs.' Ivan's voice was subtle as an axe.

'Get stuffed.' The woman snarled at him, before skulking towards the loading dock on the opposite side. Ivan slammed the door closed.

This was his opportunity.

Chapter 9

Jett snuck towards the rear door of the production facility on light feet and opened it a crack. With no sign of Ivan, he passed quickly inside. Closing the door soundlessly behind, he struggled not to cough on the remnants of tobacco smoke. Now he just had to find an office to search for evidence to prove what they were up to. If the local police didn't want to get involved, he'd go directly to the feds. And if Luca convinced them otherwise ...?

Jett suppressed this troubling possibility and took the flight of stairs to the basement. Gripping the door handle, he tried the level, but found it locked. *Man!*

Retreating back up to ground level, he knew there had to be another way to get downstairs. Bypassing multiple liquid petroleum gas cylinders, and several other cylinders labelled 'highly flammable', he absently wondered why they needed those substances.

What he really needed was a way to stop them corrupting Luca and Gen further. More so, stop them all together. His eyes fell on the service lift then drifted back to the gas cylinders. Flammable gas ... Could it work?

Jett pressed a button that brought the service lift to ground level. He opened the sliding cage protecting it, then rolled four of the large gas cylinders inside. Selecting basement, he crawled in himself. It was a tight fit, but as he expected, the lift didn't start moving until the cage gates were fully closed. Waiting for it to chug its way down and stop, he scanned the production room. The coast seemed clear, so he opened the cage gates.

As quietly as possible, he rolled the first cylinder out of the lift and moved it all the way to the back of the room. Turning back towards the service lift to relocate the next cylinder, a sealed room caught his eye. He'd missed it in his previous survey. Inside was another gas cylinder connected with tubing to what looked like a weird, computer-controlled printer—or something. It was nothing like he'd seen before.

Cautiously opening the door, he stepped inside the closed space and wiggled the computer mouse. It seemed to be mid-process. A setting in the range of nanometres was next to 'GQD size'. *GQD.* It rang a bell from his Google searches that morning. He snapped a photo of the screen and the machine, then stepped out, leaving the Perspex door open behind him.

Quickly he returned to the lift and relocated the remaining cylinders to opposite corners of the room. It was tricky navigating around equipment and benches. The effort left him in a lather.

Satisfied he had decent fire power, he wondered what he could use as an ignition source. *Smoker woman.* She had a lighter. Given she was taking a smoke break, it was unlikely she was going home. She may as well live here, with those hours! Now he just had to find her.

Jett paused near the drawer from which Ivan had produced the antidote autoinjectors. As before, the drawer was locked. *Of course.*

Breathless with urgency, he hunted for a tool he could wedge under the handle to try break the drawer open. The best he could find was a retort stand supporting a clamp guiding tubes. Loosening and removing the boss head-clamp assembly, he unscrewed the solid metal rod from the heavy base and returned to the drawer.

He fed the rod through the handle and levered hard. Seeing the inside latch starting to bend, he added greater force. With a crunch, the handle scraped out of the drawer, sending him tumbling backwards. The rod clattered onto the floor.

Heart at his teeth, Jett scrambled up and rammed

the rod into the small gap between the drawer edge and the cabinet. Levering again, he managed to break the lock, sending the drawer sliding out with a thump.

Distant voices reached him from the direction where Ivan and Gen had exited the last time he was there. This time the intonation was loud and angry. Snatching up the autoinjectors, three in total, he shoved them in his pocket.

With shaking hands, he dashed from cylinder to cylinder and opened the valves on each one. As the voices escalated, he unlocked the production room door into the stairwell and scaled the steps. Hitting the next level at full speed, he could feel adrenaline pouring through him as he paused to open the taps on the gas cylinders he'd not relocated. He then ran for the door at the rear of the building, through which he'd entered.

With the flats of his hands, he slammed the exit open, but a, 'Stop right there,' command at his back brought him to a standstill with a jolt. Ivan.

With the swinging of the door, he saw another man outside, facing him. It was the one who'd been driving the dark blue car he'd followed from the gym. A glance proved both men were armed with a gun each. His insides lurched.

'Turn around with your hands behind your head,'

Ivan ordered.

His head floated as he registered this threat. Sweat slicked his skin as he lifted his hands and laced his fingers against his hair. The man outside propped open the door and smirked.

Jett turned halfway so he could keep both men in sight. 'You've gotta stop this, Van. Luca's *crazy*.'

A smile tilted Ivan's mouth, sending a shiver down Jett's spin. 'I know. Isn't it remarkable?' Pride swelled his words.

'Gotta disagree. Why are you doing this?'

Ivan laughed, wheezing between snorts with the intensity of his amusement. 'You're too innocent, boy. We are raising an army and you're going to help us—one way, or another.'

It was the same thing he'd heard earlier. *He wants* me *to help?* 'An army, for what?'

He chuckled again. 'Ever heard of the Australian Defence Force? The Federal Police? State law enforcement?'

Jett stared. The information he'd looked up that morning ricocheted through his mind. 'What are you saying?'

'How terrible if, by some peculiar stroke of unfortunate luck, they went rogue.'

Mentally scrambling, he realised Luca had been promoting the capsules as a performance enhancer. 'You're going to recommend the capsules to those departments.'

'Smarter than you look, Jett.'

The approach of heavy footfall outside the building caught his ear.

'Van! Van, you've gotta do something.' It was Gen's voice and it held a tenor of panic. It sounded like she was sprinting. The footsteps slowed until she stopped short beside the man outside, her braids falling loose from a hasty-looking knot. 'What's with the weapons. Jett? What's going on?'

Blue-car driver turned towards her. 'Your timing is perfect, my dear. Perhaps this is just the opportunity to conduct a test of our technology?'

Jett's gaze swung from one man to the other. It felt like someone was doing macrame on his intestines.

Ivan smirked and pulled a small device from his pocket. 'Excellent idea. But do we preserve or destroy?'

Huh? The intestinal knots tightened as Gen's faintly fluorescing eyes widened.

Chapter 10

A circus troupe of thoughts trapezed through Jett's mind.

'Move. Now. You too, Gen.' Ivan's order propelled them outside.

Jett walked alongside Gen into the dark, dilapidated parking lot behind the building. Pale yellow light simpered from a single light pole looming over one corner of the area, turning her blue-dyed braids a strange hue of green. Despite dragging his feet, all too soon they were at the centre of the bitumen carpark.

'That's far enough.'

They stopped, turned, and waited for the PT to give his next directive. Ivan was standing in the rear doorway, his frame outlined by light coming from inside the building. The older, skinny, blue-car driver was standing next to the PT, as if waiting for something to happen. Jett watched Ivan raise the device he was holding to his mouth and press a button on it. Gen's eyes pulsed a rainbow spectrum and glazed over. He tensed and edged back as the strange glow returned him to his encounters with Luca.

'Jett is your enemy, Imogen. Disable him.'

Jett felt like someone was using his heart as speed-punching bag. Gen hurtled at him like a human projectile and connected hard, throwing him over. He landed heavily on the roughened surface of the car park. The small, tar-secured rocks chewed away pieces of his skin.

Before he could get up and pull a defensive move, Gen's foot connected with his side with a force that could break ribs. *Argh.* Rolling away, Jett noticed the lady who'd stepped out for a smoke was ambling back towards the door to observe the display. She pulled another cigarette from her pack and slipped it between her lips.

A moving force slammed into his head, distorting his view of the building and the people standing around the back doorway. Without pause, Gen pulled him into a headlock. He sucked in air milliseconds before she clutched one arm around his throat and gripped the back of his head with her other. If she didn't crush his trachea, he knew she could very well snap his neck. Prising at her arm with his fingers, he didn't stand a chance. With a jolt of realisation, he grappled frantically for his short's pocket.

'Shouldn't you stop her?' blue-car driver asked.

'Isn't he the challenge you wanted?'

Ivan considered this, but was clearly enjoying the scene far too much. Smoker-lady was so entranced she seemed to forget Ivan's earlier warning and lifted the lighter to her fresh cigarette.

Finally, Ivan raised the device near to his mouth. He stopped before giving further commands and sniffed the air. 'What is that smell?'

'Gen, stop,' Jett wheezed as his fingers closed around one of the autoinjectors he'd taken from the drawer in the basement facility. The pressure of her hand on his head increased as he fumbled the injector out of his pocket and blindly plucked off the cap. The cigarette lighter flared as he plunged the needle into Gen's leg to deliver the neutralising agent.

A loud whoomph preceded a thundering boom that drove him and Gen to the ground, breaking her grip on him. Bodies and bricks became airborne as the walls of the building ruptured. Gen let out a shriek and threw herself across his torso as debris rained around them. Her hands came at his neck and he braced for her fatal blow, but it stopped short. Instead, the glazed look left her eyes and she howled like a wounded animal.

Dust displaced the odour of igniting gas that had singed the air. Coughing to clear his lungs, Jett cautiously gripped Gen's shoulders and moved her off him. Watchful, he remained ready to defend himself, in case she attacked again. His side throbbed as he sat up—*has she* actually *broken ribs?*—yet the pain grew distant as he surveyed the disaster around them. Beside him, Imogen groaned and rested her forehead in her hands.

'My head. What just happened?' She looked up and blinked repeatedly, as if trying to bring the world into focus.

'You tried to kill me.' He stood and dusted off his work clothes.

Gen's eyes rounded and she gasped. 'I remember. Jett, I ... I don't know what came over me.'

'Ivan controlled your mind, just like he's planning to do with your boyfriend.'

Gen gritted her teeth. 'He's *not* my boyfriend.'

What? But the question exited his mind as she tried to stand, a sharp cry tearing from her throat. It was then he realised a large lump of bricks and mortar still pinned her leg. *Should I run while I can?*

Gen struggled to free herself, moaning in a way that suggested intense pain. Sighing, Jett relented and squatted to help. 'I'll lift. Drag your leg out.'

He bore the weight of the chunk of external wall with a grunt. Gen did as he instructed and extracted her trapped leg, but she couldn't stifle another cry as she moved. The second she was free, he let the load thud back on the bitumen. There was an odd bend in her lower leg.

'Please, don't leave me here,' she pleaded.

'Why shouldn't I? You've attacked me twice now.' His ears were muffled from the force of the explosion. Despite this, he heard the distant wail of sirens.

Gen scowled and struggled to stand. Her face twisted, betraying agony. 'I was trying to *save* you at the gym.'

Jett didn't answer as the sirens got closer. A rattle of bricks and a grunt from near the building set his head spinning. He had to get out of there. 'Fine.'

Supporting Gen under her shoulders, it took one step to prove it would be torturous to make her walk. Before he could rationalise his actions, he caught her up in his arms and carried her over the rubble that littered the space around the building.

'Where's your car?' he asked, trying not to jostle her about too much.

'I don't own a car. I use Uber.'

Jett figured it was one less thing to take care of.

By the time they reached the side-street where

he'd parked, sweat soaked his shirt and his legs and arms were heavy with fatigue. They were nearly to the car when emergency vehicles wailed past the nearby intersection, flashing lights strobing the shadowed sky. Helping Imogen into the back seat, so she could elevate and support her injury, he got into the driver's seat and turned over the engine.

As he pulled out onto the street, another rush of emergency vehicles sailed towards the ruined building. Giving way at the T-intersection, he awaited a break in traffic, ensuring he drove in the opposite direction to the destroyed production facility.

Turning onto the main road, he asked, 'Which hospital?' Pulling up at a red light, he made brief eye contact via the rear-view mirror. 'PA? Redland?'

'Jett, you're a nice guy, but you don't have to drive me. Just take me to a day-night medical centre and they can call an ambulance, if they think I need to go to emergency.'

'Your leg's broken. I don't mind, though I can't figure out why you'd take that stuff Luca's plugging. Just don't try killing me again.' To his surprise, instead of a biting rebuff, tears glistened in her eyes. 'Imogen?'

She sniffed and dropped her head. Loose braids fell across her face. He'd never seen her like this.

'I'm sorry. He ... he made me take them.'

'Both today?'

She shook her head. 'Yesterday was the first one.'

Understanding sank through Jett. 'That's why you freaked out so much this morning, when Van told you about the effect being irreversible.' It made sense why she took the antidote autoinjector.

She gulped in air and nodded. 'Luca was going crazy because I wouldn't take the damn things. I thought one mightn't hurt. But when I got to the gym this morning, after you were at the facility, he—'

'Luca?' Jett jumped as a car horn honked him from behind. He'd not even noticed the traffic lights change to green. Pressing the accelerator, he tried to keep an eye on the road, whilst attempting to read Gen's face in the snatches of brightness provided by the streetlights they passed.

'Yeah. He pinned me down, wedged my mouth open so hard he nearly broke my jaw, then shoved in a pill and plugged my mouth and nose with his hands. Said he wouldn't let go until I swallowed.' Her voice wavered as she spoke. 'Jett, he's ...' She choked down a sob.

'An out-of-control bully?' Jett finished for her, deciding to head for the Princess Alexandra Hospital. 'Is that why you stopped dating?'

She sniffed again. 'We never *were* dating. He's a touchy-feely creep, but I figured I could handle him if he tried anything dodgy. Besides, it kept the other guys away.'

Heat radiated through Jett as he considered how many times he'd wanted to tell her she should ditch Luca and hang with him. She was only eighteen months older, but she seemed to be another class above him. 'Sorry we made you uncomfortable.'

She laugh-sniffed. 'I didn't mean you. The others, though ...' She shuddered.

'You know, if I'd waited a few more seconds to inject you, that debris probably wouldn't have broken your leg, meaning you wouldn't be stuck here.' He shrugged an apology as he turned a corner.

'Yeah, but I'd have probably just as quickly smashed your head in if you'd waited, and that would've been a waste of some damn fine looks.' She caught his eye in the reflection of the mirror and attempted a smile, but it morphed into a grimace, betraying her escalating pain.

Lightness buoyed his chest, despite the seriousness of the situation. 'Is your leg hurting more?'

'Yeah, it's pretty bad.' There was a pause before she added, 'He planned to do the same to you—force you to take the pills.'

Jett remembered Ivan's interest and shivered as if someone had dumped ice on his back. He said nothing, concentrating on driving smoothly to minimise bumping Imogen around. It took forever to reach the hospital, but he grew too distracted for small talk and thick traffic made him unusually antsy. It was tempting to push the speed limit whenever he had a clear run.

'Hey, don't lose your provisional licence for me.' Gen's remark made him realise she was watching the dash over his shoulder. Yep, there was no grace when it came to "P"-platers speeding on the roads.

'Sorry. A bit keen to get there,' he admitted, resisting the urge to floor the accelerator. 'Do you need to call your folks or anyone?' He glanced back and saw her bite her lip.

'I could call them, but it wouldn't do much good. My family moved to England a couple of years ago. My only other relatives, a couple of aunts, are in WA.'

''Kay, ET's not calling home.' He caught her eye again and noticed a hint of a smile tease her mouth, but nothing could erase the growing shadow of pain darkening her face.

Tension seeped from Jett's shoulders as he pulled up in a kiss-and-drop parking space outside the emergency department. Turning off the ignition, he went to the rear passenger door to assist Imogen. Despite her insistence she could manage, no matter which way she tried, she couldn't get the right angle.

'Here, Gen. Let me.' Jett eased one arm about her shoulders and the other under her legs. Pulling her close to his body, he lifted her from the car. As he did, Gen sucked in a breath and clutched his bicep. Her blunt nails dug into his skin. 'I'm sorry,' he whispered as he cradled her in his arms. She said nothing, only leaned her head against his shoulder, as if yielding to his strength. The closeness of her did strange things to his brain.

He took Gen into the emergency department so her condition could be triaged. A wheelchair was swiftly sourced. 'I've gotta move the car, but won't be long,' he told her over the piercing cries of a small child a few chairs over.

'Jett, you don't have to stay.'

Though her words were as confident as always, uncertainty lingered in her eyes. His chest tightened and he had an unreasonable urge to draw her back inside the protection of his arms. Ivan's mind control must have really rattled her. A moment later, her phone rang.

He blinked as Gen fished around in her pocket for the mobile. *Keep it real, Jett.* He knew she'd smack him down if he dared try anything like a spontaneous embrace, even if offering comfort.

When she finally got the phone in her hand, the call had gone to message bank. As she read the caller ID, the minimal colour remaining in her face seeped to grey.

'It's Luca. He must be looking for me.' Though she tried to hide it, her hand trembled as she turned the phone off. She stared at the screen long after it had gone blank, as if needing to be certain it wouldn't spontaneously spark back to life.

Jett crouched before her and breathed away the anger combusting his reason as he thought about Luca terrorising first, Sophie, and now Imogen. 'Gen, I've gotta move the car and make a few calls to let my folks know where I am, but I'm not leaving you here alone.'

Her head came up and her eyes fastened on his. The fizz of green and rainbow no longer contaminated their slate-to-amber depths, but for all her projected independence, there was a hollowness that made Jett want to jump up and hit things. Specifically, Luca shaped things.

'I'm so not letting Luca near you again. Ever.'

'But how can you stop him?' A crease divided her brow and her gaze skirted him.

Jett's hand felt statically charged as he resisted

the urge to reach out and soothe the graceful curve of her jaw with his fingers until that haunting terror left her eyes. He didn't answer as he stood. In truth, he had no idea how to stop Luca either. But from here on he would keep the autoinjectors and capsules handy at all times.

Chapter 11

Jett navigated Imogen's wheelchair through a pair of large, automatic sliding doors, towards his car parked outside. Her leg was pinned and set, but with the break just above her ankle, the leg was only cast to her knee. She wore her workout gear from yesterday—low-waist flashdance shorts and a form-hugging white ribbed tank top that accentuated her well-carved arms and abs.

'How was your night in hospital?' he asked, careful not to unbalance the pair of crutches she had propped across the arm rests. He mentally kicked himself for not offering to get her a fresh change of clothes.

'Not so bad, due to these amaaaazing things called drugs. I barely remember the surgery this morning.' She gave an uncharacteristic giggle, betraying she was still affected by said pharmaceuticals.

He'd come as soon as he could after a quick post-work shower, insisting she let him drive her home. Planning ahead, he'd done a vehicle swap with his mum, figuring her larger SUV would allow more room to accommodate Gen's newly set leg. At the car he locked the wheelchair wheels, opened wide the car door, then pushed back the front seat as far as it would go. With some manoeuvring, he managed to assist Gen from the chair, into the vehicle. With her arms still linked about his neck, he adjusted her seat to ensure she was reasonably comfortable.

'I might have to keep you around for a while as my personal mobility aid,' she giggled, arms lingering. When she didn't let go, Jett unclasped her fingers and eased her away so she could clip herself in. His skin was alight where her hands had been.

Unlike their trip to the hospital, Gen talked. A lot. More than she ever had. Her monologue drifted seamlessly from one unrelated topic to the next.

'Know what the girls at the gym call you?' she asked, her words running together slightly. 'Channing.'

Jett frowned, though he kept his eyes on the traffic. 'As in the actor, Channing Tatum?'

'Yeah, 'cos you're all chiselled and *hot*, and you do kinda look like him, just with funkier hair.'

'Not really.'

'Yeah, you do, *'specially* when he was younger. Oh yeah, a lotta gym girls have asked for *your* number, Jett. You could have *any* girl you want.'

Jett's skin was instantly prickly. 'I'm not really interested in having "any girl I want",' he said, thinking how ironic it was that the one girl he was interested in was sitting next to him drivelling words more than a person with no teeth.

She twisted in her seat and poked his arm, a goofy grin decorating her face. 'That's what makes you even *more* attractive. You've got principles. An' my dad says, "Principles are what make a boy a man".'

'I think I'd like your dad,' Jett said, grinning.

'Yeah, but he's all stuffy an' religious.' She flopped her hand through the air.

Her words arrowed into Jett's soul and his smile dulled. After a slight pause, he clarified, 'Religious? As in a Jesus kinda way?'

'Yep, one o' them, like ...' Eyes darting to his, her face turned a pink that contrasted her bold hair colour. 'You're one, aren't you?'

'Yep.' His grin returned as she slapped her forehead with her palm. Trying not to laugh, he asked, 'Just how much morphine did they give you?'

'A bit. Why?'

He shrugged. 'No reason.'

'What?'

'I've just never seen this side of you,' he admitted.

Immediately, her fist connected with his shoulder. 'Ow! What was that for?'

'Figured it was a side you were better acquainted with,' she said, laughing.

'For that, you owe me. And I have the perfect way to pay you back.' He glanced at her and saw her face scrunch.

'Wait, do I owe you or you owe me? That made no sense.'

'Like you, right now,' he muttered under his breath, only to receive another thump. 'Will you stop that?' Gen only laughed.

Abruptly her chatter ceased. At first Jett figured she'd run out of steam, but a sideward glance told him she'd fallen asleep. If it weren't so dangerous, he would have watched her all the way home.

With superhuman effort he dragged his eyes away from the adorable freckles dotting her nose and the cinnamon lashes fanned above her cheeks. Those high cheek bones of hers always depicted an air of sophistication—even when she was lathered in sweat, fist up in victory at the end of a fight.

Being this close to her made Jett float like a helium balloon. She seemed so harmless as she slept. He clamped down a smile. How looks could be deceiving.

Gen stirred again when they were nearly to her house. With the last smudge of orange leaving the sky, he made an impulsive diversion. He knew the perfect way to pay her back.

'Gen, you awake?'

She gave a soft moan. 'No.'

'I have an idea. You up for ice cream?'

A groggy giggle escaped her. 'You and ice cream. Sure.'

'Hey, it was a hot day, not that *you'd* know. Besides, isn't that the appropriate food for someone after an operation?'

She snorted. 'I didn't have my tonsils out.'

'Hey, I'm not prejudiced. An operation is an operation,' he said, pulling up at a local ice creamery. 'What's your fav?'

'Anything salted caramel or nut fudge in a waffle cone.'

'Gotcha. Back in a min.'

Gen was still sluggish when he returned to the car. Carefully he passed her their ice creams to hold, before driving the short distance to the waterfront. Parking so they could watch the ocean, he lowered the windows so the cool, salty breeze could blow in on them.

'Is this a date?' She licked a dribble of ice cream

from the side of the cone. 'Mmmm, this is good.'

'I know, right? And no, it's not a date. This is payback. Remember?'

'I should hit you more often then.'

Inferno-worthy heat scorched Jett's face, but he hoped she wouldn't notice. What he *really* wanted to say was unequivocally 'yes, this is a date, and it will be the first of many dates, if you'll let me take you out'. But that was a pipe dream. Gen had never given any indication she was interested in anything more than friendship with him, and even that was a stretch. More like, casual acquaintances. Besides, from their conversation he'd realised their values were polar opposites when it came to relationships. He changed the topic.

'So, how much do you know about this performance enhancing mind control stuff? What's the point of trialling this on Luca and his recruits, only to use it to send our frontline defence force rogue?' It proved the perfect segue to killing any hint of romance.

For a moment Gen kept eating her ice cream. He waited as she crunched down a piece of cone. A resigned sigh followed. 'Like Ivan says, he's raising an army.'

'But why?'

She took another bite, chewed, and swallowed. 'Don't know exactly, but I heard him and Sean talking—'

'Sean?'

'The older guy. They were saying the best way to effect an invasion without firing a shot, is to take the citizens of a country hostage by their own protectors.'

Jett surveyed the water. For the first time in his life he felt nauseous while eating ice cream. He'd seen how easily Ivan had manipulated Imogen with a simple signal. This information dripped through his mind, much like the melted ice cream trickling down the outside of his half-eaten cone.

'So, what you're saying is if the local law and military forces turn on Australia's own citizens, the people would be so grateful for intervention, they would happily trade their freedoms for protection by, say, an invading force?'

'That'd be my guess. And before you ask, I have no idea if that would be a specific foreign nation, a global organisation, or other.'

After spending long hours last night trying to figure out how the technology worked, he'd decided there were two or three likely mechanisms in play. The fluorescence seemed to occur when the enhanced person was agitated, excited or threatened. Based on his readings, he guessed either heat or a biochemical interaction triggered the superhuman strength and weirdo glow. The term he'd found linked to this was 'chemogenetics'.

He'd then searched up fluorescent substances matching the formulas on the whiteboard. That was harder. It had been several years since he'd done any chemistry, but the closest he found was nanoparticle quantum dots—QDS—like on the machine in the sealed room. Interestingly, QDS uses include neuromodulation through what's called optoelectronic neural interfacing.

Further digging into the diagram he'd photographed in the production room suggested the light emitted by these particles might trigger another pathway—termed optogenetics—linking the two activated pathways to control and enhance certain behaviours. By the time he'd closed down the computer his brain was like mashed potato.

If he had to guess what behaviours were being enhanced, aggression and a positive association with power and control seemed high on the list. Then again, maybe that was just Luca's unique brand of charm. Something else he'd read said these signals could be changed to cause a test subject to forget the associated trigger, or even other memories, in a way reversing the effect. From what Ivan said, he wasn't sure if this was possible. Somehow in this puzzle fit the mysterious modified magneto protein.

Finishing his ice cream, he wiped his hands and mouth with the serviette supplied by the ice creamery. He looked to Gen. 'Ready to go home?'

She met his gaze with wide, uncertain eyes, deep with unspoken emotion. 'Can we just sit for a while? Unless I'm keeping you up after your bedtime.' Her eyes curved as she teased him.

'Nah, it's the weekend tomorrow. I might even be able to stay out 'til eight. Let me call Mum to check it's okay.'

Gen laughed and pointed through the windscreen. 'Jett, see that bench along the water?' His line-of-sight followed her finger. 'Could you carry me to it?'

His eyes shot back to hers. 'That's gonna hurt. Sure you're not in too much pain? You'll have to get shuffled around again at your house.'

'I'm sure. And I've got more drugs, if I need.'

'I still don't think moving you is the best idea.' *Correction—me carrying you is a really* terrible *idea.* But her hopeful expression swayed him.

Exiting the car, he went to the passenger side and opened the door. Gen stuck out her hand with dramatic flair, like some Prima donna rockstar, but as he took her fingers in his, Jett was struck by the daintiness of them, especially for someone so capable of taking down a guy. Leaning in, he assisted in swivelling her set leg out the door, before getting in close to lift her.

Jett slid one arm under her knees. The cast rasped against his wrist, but he barely noticed due to the way his heartrate surged as he placed his other arm at Gen's back and drew her into his chest. Despite being fresh out of hospital, her braids were surprisingly smooth as they brushed against his cheek. *Stupid, stupid idea.* He kept repeating this to himself, but as Gen wrapped her arms about his neck, Jett felt like he'd dived into deep ocean water and was now adrift in forceful, foaming waves.

'Ready?' he asked, trying to not sound like he was under siege, but he couldn't think straight this near to her. This was different to the frantic moments following the explosion at the production facility, when he'd carried her to the car. So, so, different.

At Gen's nod, he lifted her from the seat and carried her the short distance to the waterfront. As he went to place her on the bench at the water's edge, she tipped up her face so their noses were nearly touching. He smiled into her eyes, noticing how the slate colouring of her irises seemed darker in the light of dusk, making the amber ring around her pupils more prominent.

Before he could guess her intention, her arm and back muscles flexed as she pulled herself higher in his arms and kissed him softly on the mouth.

Hand finding the back of his neck, she curled into him and whispered against his throat, 'Thank you for everything.'

Caught off guard, he nearly dropped her.

Chapter 12

With an ungraceful recovery, Jett plopped down onto the bench with Gen on his lap. Sensible words were dust to the wind and his entire body felt electrified. Gen placed the flat of her palm against his chest, directly over his careening heart, while her fingertips traced his face, drawing invisible lines of fire from his cheek down to the light stubble prickling his jaw.

He inhaled shakily. 'Gen, you're still feeling the effects of those pain killers. We're just friends, and barely that.'

'Jett, I know exactly what I'm doing.'

'I don't think yo—'

Her lips were soft and still cold from the ice cream as they apprehended his. Jett found himself kissing her back with a growing intensity he'd never imagined between them. Before he could figure out which side was up, Gen's mouth was moving against his neck in a way that could make a guy self-combust. *Smokin' snapdragons.*

Pulling back abruptly, he sat her on the bench next to him, putting some distance between them.

'What's wrong? You don't like me kissing you?'

'Never said that,' he mumbled, scraping his hands down his face. Blood roared through him and he was breathing like he'd just finished bench-pressing his PB. 'I'm as human as the next guy, Gen, but this is crazy. I've gotta get you home.' He also didn't feel right about leaving her alone against post-operative advice. 'Are you *sure* you don't want to call someone to help you out?'

Her eyes sparkled and she placed her palm, like a live coal, atop his quad. '*You* could stay.'

'Yep, definitely too much morphine,' he joked, easing out from under her touch, only to have her capture his hand and hold it to her throat. He could feel her pulse strong under his fingers. 'And what about your leg, remember?'

'I have these amazing drugs, remember?' Gen studied him. Abruptly, all hints of teasing faded and tears shimmered in her eyes. 'Are you sure you're okay? I nearly killed you yesterday.'

He slid his hand up her neck, to her jaw, and charted the curve of her cheek with his thumb. She shivered as he did. 'Imogen, it's okay. I'm fine. Just a few bruises.'

'But what if the neutraliser hadn't worked?'

He levelled his gaze on her. 'It did. End of story.' Unable to resist, he cradled her back against his chest. Gen sighed and relaxed into him. Sparks flew through him once more.

'I still can't believe Luca forced that pill down my throat. He kept saying it wouldn't take long to feel the effects, that it'd be even better than the first, and when it hit, I'd be thanking him.'

Jett frowned at the water and rested his chin at her temple. It was typical abuser talk. 'How long before the effects kicked in?'

She shook her head, her hair tickling his neck. 'In hours. He said with each repeat dose, the invincibility would increase until it reached saturation.'

'And how long until you became a remote-control robot?' he rasped, unable to shut down the snapshots of her attack that rammed through his mind.

'If I understand correctly, there are two steps in the process, which start taking effect a day or so after the first dose. The first involves self-assembling superparamagnetic particles, creating a transhuman nanotechnology network for signal transmission and biodata monitoring.'

Wait on. Jett frowned as questions snap-froze his

gut, like a swallowed lump of dry ice. His late-night reading on normal magneto proteins had shown they could be used to open certain protein channels directly into neural cells, or other targets—like the cell membrane diagram he'd seen on the board. This also allowed behaviour modification. Gen's detailed description of *how* this occurred unsettled him like a burr in his shorts.

Squaring his shoulders, he drew away. 'Can you repeat that, in English?'

'Superparamagnetic QDS particles are in the pills. When ingested, they redistribute around the body, connecting to each other to create a network that can enable signals to be sent and received, and information about the "host" remotely monitored.'

Jett blinked, feeling like someone had just king-hit him in the chest. Was this what the 'modified' part of 'modified magneto' referred to? He'd figured by the way Ivan had 'remote controlled' Gen, it had something to do with radio waves or electromagnetic signals being somehow received from the controller, but she was talking casually about highly sophisticated technology he had no hope of comprehending. 'How do you know this stuff?'

As if suddenly shy, she pressed her fingers one-by-one against the metal slats of the bench, before allowing her gaze to creep up and meet Jett's own. 'I'm a biophysicist by trade and in the army reserve.'

'What? How? You're only twenty.'

Gen's eyes skated away. 'Yeah, um, I did most of an accelerated bachelor's degree at high school and am halfway through my masters. I got involved with Van through my military training and sought out his advice to help me go pro with Muay Thai.'

She turned away and stared across the water. Jett noticed a shudder run over her.

'That still doesn't explain *how* you know that stuff you just told me.'

Gen shrugged. 'I ... ah ... had some special ops training. Was looking for work. Didn't take long for him to recruit my help—trade my expertise for his, with a monster bonus. But recently it's become clear he lied about his intentions.'

Limbs hanging as if packed with sand, Jett sucked in a lungful of air and slowly let it out. There it was. Gen had helped facilitate this mess. Whether it was ignorance as she claimed, clearly, she still had enough of a relationship with Van to feel free to visit the site, ask questions, and remain associated.

'And the second?'

Her face pivoted toward him. 'Huh?'

'You said there were two mechanisms.'

'Oh, right. The particle biodistribution carries genetic fragments that tell the body to produce regulating structures that integrate with key neural pathways and the quantum material, allowing behavioural modification.'

Translation—the technology can genetically modify someone so their body makes proteins that allow their behaviour to be controlled. Awesome.

A small line creased her brow. 'He said the fluorescence is evidence of successful protein expression and function and is only being used for the trials. Given it's a unique quantum particle feature and a trigger for linked pathways, I don't know what he's planning on replacing it with, once the concept's proven. Maybe a luminescence invisible to the naked eye?'

Gen's eyelids fluttered and she leaned into him. Absorbing this reality, Jett felt like he was holding a serpent. If either Sean or Ivan had survived the explosion—and despite no specific news, there was no evidence they hadn't—Luca could become even more weaponised, if that were possible. *And Gen.*

'Jett, although I'm familiar with those biophysical properties of the technology, during development we were each kept in our own corner, so to speak. They told me the technology was a prototype for internal biometric monitoring that would ultimately lead to vital medical advances. I'm inferring much of what I've told you based on recent observations and conversations I've overheard between Sean and Van, plus the limited details they've chosen to share.'

Jett stiffened at this claim. 'It seems to me you've been more involved than some "limited details" relating to your corner of the project.'

Her eyes pleaded as she reached out and wrapped her fingers about his wrist. 'I honestly didn't get it at the time. As Luca became more … terrifying—' Her whole body juddered. '—It freaked me out enough to question their "program". That's why I went with Sean that morning to the factory. I wanted answers.'

He twisted out of her hold, knowing she could stop him from doing so, if she really wanted to. Instead, she folded her hands together on her lap, looking smaller and more vulnerable than he could have imagined possible.

'I swear, Jett, my gut-deep fear they were going for something more nefarious was only confirmed when they weaponised me against you. I was conscious of myself, of you, but I couldn't defy Van's orders.'

All too aware of his weakness when it came to resisting her, he settled his focus on the water—anywhere, but Gen. 'I don't know how you think I'm supposed to trust you now?'

'Van claimed it was being validated in conjunction with a performance modification supplement as a health-augmenting tool. I didn't know.'

'If that's true, they're gonna figure out you're not onboard soon enough.' Even as he spoke, doubt blemished his confidence in her claim. 'What'll you do if Luca or Ivan come after you?'

She scoffed, a broken half-laugh, half-cry. Jett's rebellious eyes sought her out as she shrugged and faced up to him. 'I don't know. Somehow, I doubt the police would take my claims very seriously if I tried to get a restraining order.'

'Or Luca would find a way to turn it back on you,' Jett muttered, a bitter taste at the back of his throat.

'Gen, I still don't see how you didn't figure the risk of taking the pills when you knew the technology they'd developed, but if you're serious about breaking free and either of them come near you, call me straight up.'

Her face softened, warming her gaze in a way that invited him closer. 'Thank you. And for the record, I think we're a little *more* than friends, at this point.' As if daring him, one eyebrow edged up and she tilted her face, a pert smile angling her mouth.

Flip. He was like a man on quicksand, needing to lay flat and still to prevent being sucked down. *Don't move, don't move, don't—*

Her eyes were magnets and he leaned in, breath dancing in anticipation. Sinking fast, his resolve melted away as he was submerged by a powerful attraction.

Despite his better judgement, he brushed his lips against hers, setting them ablaze. Before he could anticipate it, Gen slid up against him, closing their distance to nothing—how, with her leg, he didn't know. She wrapped her arms around his neck and pressed her mouth fiercely to his, sending his stomach into a backflip. *Crickey!* Her lips were ravenous, as his own craving possessed him.

By the time they paused, Jett's head felt detached and his body hummed. Breathing heavily, he couldn't form a sentence to save himself. All he knew was he'd never been kissed by a girl in that way before. Mentally scrambling for words, he finally managed to cobble together some sense.

'Gen, what are we doing?' His voice was hoarse and his pulse hammered in his throat.

'Stay with me tonight,' she murmured against his mouth.

Reality slogged him in the face like a tub of ice cream. He jerked away, putting more space between them than before. There it was—the cavern between them. 'Gen, I ... I can't do that. *Won't* do that.'

Hardness darkened her face and her eyes narrowed. 'Seriously? *Now* you find your *principles*.' She folded her arms like a shield.

'Look, this was a mistake. I shouldn't have let things go this way. It's not fair on either of us.'

'Jett, you can't deny we have crazy-good chemistry.' She inched closer. He inched back the same measure. 'Come back to my place. No one needs to know.'

'Gen, *I'll* know.' He forced out a breath and let his shoulders round. 'I can't say I didn't enjoy kissing you—probably too much—and I'd not object to doing it again. But what then? We barely know each other.'

'Who cares. You're insanely hot. Everyone has a body count.'

Jett stoppered a groan. 'Gen, I'm more than my looks; my body.'

'But it sure makes for pretty fine eye candy.' She chewed on the edge of her upper lip and gave him a look that could melt steel.

'Um, that's … flattering.' Honestly, he hated that this was all most girls saw in him. He rubbed the back of his head with his hand. 'But so are you—more than looks, I mean. You're a class act, and every time you step into a room it's like everything else fades to grey.'

Her eyes softened. 'That's got to be the nicest thing anyone's said about me in a long time.'

Jett's eyes fastened on hers, as if searching her soul. 'I'd like get to know you beyond the mega crush I've been nursing for nearly a year, and let you see who I am, other than my appearance.'

'A year, huh?' Her mouth hitched at the corner in a half-smile.

'Pretty much.'

'Okay, so … what would you tell me?'

'I've got this addiction.' As he spoke, her eyebrows rose in question. 'I'm kinda useless when it comes to resisting ice cream.' *And you*, he added silently as she laughed.

'I might have heard that somewhere already. What else?'

'Well … my "principles" aren't an optional extra I pick up when it's convenient.'

Gen rolled her head and groaned, briefly turning her eyes to the sky. 'I just think you're taking it a bit far.

I heard somewhere it's not good for man to be alone.' She angled her body towards him, the invitation in her smoky eyes obvious.

Jett glanced away, his face flashing hot. 'It matters to me.' He knew she'd think it was lame, but he had to be honest. Fixing his gaze on hers, he said, 'I'm *known*, Gen, and loved. Even when I'm a total mess up.'

Gen gave a derisive laugh. 'I don't think you even know what messing up looks like.'

'Actually, I do—way more than anyone knows. And voiding my blame for those screw-ups came at a high price. I don't want to dishonour that, even in this … thing …' He waved his hand back and forth from him to her, making up for words he couldn't find. '… Happening between us. Because you're known, too.'

She drew back, distancing herself, and smacked her lips. 'That, ah, was quite the high-road speech. I … ah, don't know what to say to that, but I still think you're taking it too liter- …' All at once her focus darted to a point behind him, her gaze orb-like. 'Jett!'

Something hit him in the centre of his back with the force of a wrecking ball. It dropped him off the bench onto the grass, his body convulsing. He heard Gen cry out in pain, then start shrieking.

'Luca, what have you done? Is that a stun gun?'

Jett scrambled to get himself together, but his head felt like a super bouncy ball tossed into a skate bowl. He was aware of footsteps and heavy breathing. Before he could get his limbs in order, another bolt lanced through his neck, longer and harder than the first.

'Stop! Luca. You'll kill him.'

'You're *my* babe,' he snarled. 'And you're going to *keep* being *my* girl.'

'Luca, I'm not your girl. You know that. Jett. Help!'

A third shock hit him. All he could do was lie face down on the ground writhing while Gen's pleas abruptly stopped, as if erased like a forgotten dream. The mind searing charge stopped. His body ceased moving. And the world faded into a disjointed vacuum, as if stretched across multiple dimensions.

Chapter 13

'Jett? What are you doing?'

Jett raised his head and blinked. *Argh.* Car lights lit up a silhouette darting across the nature strip towards him. 'Soph?' Instantly his twin was beside him, assisting him up.

'What happened?' Alarm sharpened her words as she eased him onto the park bench where he and Gen had been sitting. Every muscle in his body whined. 'Weren't you supposed to be taking your friend home from hospital?'

He groaned and, elbows on knees, cradled his head in his palms. 'Gen.'

'Gen? Who's that?'

'Luca attacked me. I think. And Gen.'

'What do you mean by "attacked"?' Sophie sank down beside him and clasped his wrist. 'Jett, you're not making sense. If Luca's got anything to do with this, you need to report him to the police.'

But Gen ... 'You don't understand. He's out of

control.'

'All the more reason.' She gave his arm a gentle shake, as if that could cover the fear warping her voice. 'What did he do to you?'

'I *think* he tasered me.'

She jumped up and dug her phone from her pocket. 'I'm dialling crime stoppers.'

'No, Soph—' But she wasn't listening and went ahead with reporting Luca for assault.

'Was anyone else involved?' she hissed, holding the phone away from her mouth.

'Gen,' he admitted quietly. Where would Luca have taken her?

'My brother's friend was here, but she seems to be gone now. I'm sure he can come down to the station to make a statement. Thanks.' She ignored Jett's hand slashing a hard horizontal line of refusal in the air and hung up.

'I'm not making a statement, Soph. He's dangerous. And he's got Gen.'

'Who's Gen?'

'Imogen Gale.' He glanced up at her sharp intake of breath.

'The Muay Thai champion? You're friends with ...?' Sophie's eyes rounded, then snapped into tight, penetrating beads. 'Wait a minute. That was *you* making out on this bench just before?'

Of *course* she knew. 'It's nothing. And how did you see us anyway?'

'Didn't *look* like nothing.' A smirk twisted her mouth. 'I was going home from the gym. Thought it looked like Mum's SUV parked here, but it was pretty dark and I got distracted by this couple trying to swallow each other on the park bench. Isn't Imogen, like, two years older than us?'

'Shut up. And it's more like eighteen months.'

'Jett and Imogen, sitting in a tree—'

'Stop it, Soph.'

'Last I heard, she was *Luca's* girlfriend. Now you're doing tongue tango with her like some Romeo wanna be?'

'And for that Luca did this.' Inside him helplessness and humiliation performed a dangerous sword dance. 'F-Y-I she kissed me first.'

Sophie offered a guttural snort from the back of her throat. 'Didn't look like you were trying to fend her off much.'

'I didn't mean it like that.'

Skin scorching, he stood in the hope it might confront her into silence. It didn't.

'Then why did you let her kiss you?'

'Because ...' Jett felt near to melting. '... Because I've had this idiotic crush on her for ages.'

Sophie's mouth dropped and her eyes rounded. 'Why didn't you ever say anything? It looked pretty ... intense.'

He blew out air and mumbled, 'Tell me about it.'

'You could've told me.'

He shrugged. 'It's not like I'm gonna announce it every time I like a girl—just like you don't with Blaine.'

'Fair.' She bit her bottom lip and broke eye contact.

Jett knew he'd struck a tender point. Honestly, he wished Blaine would just make his move. The guy was seriously into his sister. But he also got things were hugely complicated between them, especially with his mate's ongoing health issues and Sophie's unstoppable determination to get a PhD and find a cure. He slung his arm around her shoulders. 'Hey, it'll work out.'

Returning his side hug, she leaned her head against his shoulder. 'I hope so. And good thing I came looking when Mum asked if I knew where you were. You know she and Dad are going to a work Christmas party tonight?'

Slowly Jett's mind grew less fragmented. As they

stepped apart his hand lingered briefly on her shoulder to show his gratitude. 'Thanks for coming, sis, but this is a major fail and I don't know how to fix it.' He was desperate for her to understand the urgency. 'He could really hurt her, permanently, and with his enhancement there's no way the police will be able to stop him.'

'I don't agree. It's just steroids, right?'

And some. He let the comment pass.

'Jett, the police need to be involved. Was it Senior Constable Gassmann who pinged you at the gym? Maybe give him a call to set the record straight.'

He nodded. She was right. But only *after* Luca was returned to his subnormal status. A plan took shape in his mind. Maybe he *did* know how to stop Luca for good.

'Hey, can I ask a fav?'

'Maybe ...' Sophie's eyes thinned. Even in the dark they held laser-like intensity.

'I need you to cover for me this weekend. I'm gonna lay low.'

'And do what?' she demanded. 'Hunt Luca down? No way.'

'Not hunt, just locate. But if I don't get home by Sunday afternoon, call the police and keep away from Luca ... and ... and me.'

Distress flared like a torch across her face. 'What

are you talking about? I don't understand what you mean, but you're scaring me.'

He hugged her properly then steered them both towards their cars. Knowing what this could do to his family was a sucker punch to his gut, but he had to cover. Sophie had enough going on in without him creating more drama. 'Don't worry, Soph. I'll explain later, but you'll have to trust me.'

She huffed out a breath and eyed him askance as they diverted to their respective vehicles. 'You're seriously becoming too much like Blaine. By the way, did you call him, like you said?'

'Don't change the topic. Yes, but I had to leave a message. And if I were Blaine, I wouldn't be asking for a backup plan,' he said with a crooked smile.

Sophie returned it grudgingly. 'True. Fine. I'll cover. But if Luca as much as shows his nose, he's gone.'

'Thanks, Soph. Seriously though, don't go anywhere near him. And if he comes to the house, get *everyone* away.' In reality his sister's threat was idle, but this time Jett was determined his would not be. It was way over time he dropped his nice guy persona and stood up against the creeps of the gym world.

Don't take them all at once. Luca's warning reverberated in Jett's mind as he stood in the middle of his bedroom and stared at the glow-in-the-dark capsules. If he took them now, in just hours he should be fully enhanced. And on the off-chance Ivan or Sean were still lurking about, he hoped Imogen was right about the delay on remote controllability. It also occurred to him that his capacity to stay calm under pressure might be a major advantage.

Perhaps being a nice guy had a benefit after all, when it came to retaining control. In which case, he hoped it would help him defeat Luca once and for all. He also realised this was the end of his bodybuilding ambitions. It would be wrong to compete with such an advantage. Gen and his family—not to mention Australia—were more important.

Here goes.

The capsules were bitter in his mouth. Jett gulped mouthfuls of water from the bottle in his gym kit. *Bleh.* He nearly gagged as the pills stuck in his throat. Taking another guzzle of water, he finally got them down far enough not to vomit.

'Honey, when did you decide this?'

Jett spun around as the door to his room opened. His heartrate ratcheted into overdrive as he swiped dribbled water from his mouth. 'Mum! You scared me.'

She was wearing a party dress and had her hair and make-up done.

'Sorry, but I saw your note. When did you decide to go camping with friends? Isn't it a bit late to head off tonight?'

He'd hoped she'd only see the note *after* he'd left, meaning he could dodge any questions and avoid lying to her face. 'It's a last-minute thing.' He tried not to wince at his vagueness. It would only make her more suspicious.

'Where are you going?'

He shrugged. 'Maybe Straddie?' *Maybe not …*

'Stradbroke Island? But you don't know for sure? Who's organising it?'

His stomach twisted enough to join a yogalates class and he fought to keep his face neutral. 'Look, Mum, I just need to clear my head. This whole gym thing's got me more worked up than I'd thought. I'm sorry for the lack of warning, but it's important.'

A smile hitched one side of her mouth. 'Yes, Sophie mentioned your hangout this afternoon. All you told us was you were picking up a gym friend, not a *girl*friend.'

Seriously, Soph? His body blistered with heat. 'It's nothing, Mum. She was still a bit drugged out after her operation and things got overly friendly.'

A frown dimpled her forehead. 'It's not like you to keep secrets, Jett. You'd let me know if anything was wrong?'

He gave her a quick hug. 'Mum, I've got to do this, okay? Gotta clear my head.'

'Okay. Dad and I are heading off now. Love you.'

'Love you, too. Enjoy your party.'

She left the room and he pulled out his backpack. Taking the two remaining autoinjectors from where he'd hidden them, he stuffed them in his Velcro-sealed shorts pocket and shoved a change of clothes into a backpack— just in case Mum checked him on the way out. Closing the zipper, he grabbed his phone and slid it into his back pocket. It was time to get moving.

Chapter 14

The night air was warm and still—a direct conflict to the cyclonic emotions that stormed through Jett as he pedalled his mountain bike to his old gym. He figured it was a logical first place to look for Luca and Gen. Arriving, he dumped the bike behind the building, shrugged off the backpack, and searched out the side entry. Unlocked. Sweet.

Stealing inside, he heard a boxercise class in progress in one of the group session rooms, while in the resistance training area, several guys he knew were doing weights. Nothing out of the ordinary.

Further along, the lights were off in Luca's office. A check of the door confirmed it was locked. Where could he have taken Gen?

Helplessness crashed through him like an internal tsunami. Retracing his path, he stepped out the side-door through which he'd entered and returned to the place he'd left his bike. It was gone. Glancing around, the hairs on his body bristled as he sensed a presence behind him.

'Looking for me, Jetto?'

Luca. Spiralling about 180 degrees, with narrowed gaze, he threw himself at the man, slamming him into the external brick wall of the building. 'What have you done with her?'

Luca's lips tilted in a crooked line, as if he didn't care less that Jett had him pinned. 'I couldn't ask *you* a better question.'

Jett's mouth turned dry. 'What are you talking about? *You're* the one who took Gen *and* threatened my sister.'

A smirk gnarled across Luca's mouth. 'What's your problem, Jetto? What happened to the easy-going church mouse?'

'He got sick of being pushed around by a jerk.'

With a flare of rainbow and green, Luca flexed his muscles and shrugged Jett off like a sweat-soaked towel. 'Seems your overinflated standards have gone to your head. Should've taken up my offer for help.' He pushed Jett back with the flat of his palms, landing him on the ground. 'Why don't you pick on someone your own size?'

Uncertainty sprinkled through him as he raised himself off the ground. There was something about Luca's tone that made his stomach clench. 'I didn't pick on *anyone*. What have you done with Imogen?'

'I've got nothing to explain to the police when they get here, unlike *you*.'

'*What?* I didn't do anything wrong.' Jett's heart pounded like a baseline from his workout playlist.

'That's not the way she tells it. Hey, babe?'

Babe?

As if on cue, Imogen stepped outside, through the door where he'd passed moments earlier. He felt untethered as he tried to figure out what was going on.

'You're a two-faced creep, Jett.' Her voice broke.

It seemed his insides were funnelling out his feet, like a washing machine purging water. Gen came up behind Luca, huddling into his shoulder as if she were at risk. Her cast was gone. Hadn't her leg been broken?

'You always seemed so nice, but you're just a pious pretender.'

'Gen, you're not remembering properly.' The washing machine flicked to spin, making his stomach heave.

'Except, Jetto, it was all recorded on video.'

Before he could argue Luca's claim, Gen started backing away. It was then Jett became aware of red and blue flashing lights closing in on them.

Luca's face twisted into a snarl that rivalled an

aggravated Tasmanian Devil. 'You've got nowhere to hide, Jetto.'

Police officers spilled out squad car doors and formed a defensive line. Pointing at him, Imogen shouted an accusation. 'He forced me to kiss him and ... and ... pervert!'

What? No!

'Jett Faraday? Hands in the air.' Police? A voice he recognised—Senior Constable Gassmann—then declared to the world he was under arrest for assault involving licentious acts against Imogen.

Anger flared inside him. Had Gen set him up— *used* him—for Luca's revenge? Had she faked a broken leg just to suck him in? It didn't seem possible, but given her intimate knowledge of the capsule's formulation ... *She played me.*

A strange ringing started in his ears as the police rushed in, yanked his hands behind his back, and cuffed him. Head down so he didn't have to look at Luca's conniving face, his eyes distorted and the grass next to the cement path became so clear he could see the tiny hairs on each leaf. Raising his head, it was like someone had turned on a light, bringing such clarity that the night became like day.

'Burn in hell, Jett,' Luca spat, as the police turned

him around and marched him towards a paddy wagon. 'Come on, babe. Let's go.'

In the same way the gas had ignited at the production factory, anger erupted in a war cry. Squeezing his eyes shut, he shrugged off the police officers either side of him and snapped the handcuffs off his wrists like plastic. He pressed his hands against his ears to block out the surrounding sounds. It was like every noise was amplified a hundred times.

'Jett, get in the car,' Gassmann ordered as hands pulled at his arms, trying to haul him into the vehicle.

'Sir, what's going on?' one policewoman asked.

'He's glowing?' said another officer.

Jett didn't need to fight them. Passive resistance was enough. Each breath hit his lungs with an efficiency that translated into a supercharged rush of power. He could feel his muscles increasing in volume as if pumped up thrice their usual post-workout size. With another animalistic roar, he opened his eyes. It didn't even sound like his voice. He could hear the police whispering amongst themselves.

'What's happening?'

'Sir?'

'Subdue him and bring him into custody.'

Jett glared as they reached for their sides. Taser?

Gun? Bring it on. He was confident he could withstand anything. He felt invincible, yet equally out of control. Backing towards Luca and Gen, he shouted, 'I did *not* assault Imogen Gale. Luca's a liar. *He's* the attacker.'

The police officers hurried after him, but he sped up. Running backwards was somehow a breeze. Suddenly the police officers skidded to a stop. Eyes wide, they stared at him and then a point behind him. Jett sensed movement at his back.

'It's your word against ours, Jett,' Luca growled.

Jett could feel him just a few steps behind; could hear each lurching breath, and knew he was getting to Luca. It wouldn't take much to tip him over. 'Luca, I don't know what you've done to Imogen, but if it's all recorded on video like you claim, then the police know you're a fraud, a liar, and a cheat.'

'*No* one calls me a liar.'

'You're a baby and a bully.' Jett felt the pulse of energy as Luca's reaction triggered the fluorescence-linked pathway.

'Sir, they're both glowing,' one of the police officers said without lowering her weapon.

In seconds a force collided with Jett's back. He crashed to the ground and twisted about to meet this attack. Luca was fluorescing even more than him. No wonder the police weren't moving. He was also much stronger than Jett had anticipated, yet he felt no fear. Empowered, it was like nothing could hurt him. And maybe it couldn't.

'Fall back, fall back. Get the woman out of here.'

Jett realised he was losing control because of his rage at Luca. He had to rein himself in, otherwise he'd have no hope of outsmarting the man. And what about Gen?

Betrayal savaged his last fragments of reason, but he fought against it. As this reality squeezed his mind, the urge to destroy Luca became overpowering. *Got. To. Get. Control.*

Jett dropped to his knees, shut his eyes, and forced Luca from his mind. He focussed on his parents, sisters, friends. He had to do this for his family, for the whole country, maybe even the world. *And Gen?*

Lifting his head, he locked eyes with her. Even as Luca's knee slammed into his head with crushing force, he maintained eye contact as he toppled sidewards, searching for truth. A green-dominated rainbow shimmered in her eyes.

They'd reactivated her. *That's* how her broken leg had miraculously healed. Doubt over her degree of involvement and motivation lingered like week-old fish guts. He clutched at the possibility Ivan may have also used the technology to create altered versions of reality for her, or even new memories. This was something he'd read about during his research, but recognised his mental overreach to rationalise her soul-searing sell-out. Either way, this meant Ivan or Sean, or both, were still alive.

As Jett buckled to the ground, Luca tried kicking him in the side. Each time the enraged man struck out, Jett rolled away, avoiding contact by a shave. He felt detached from reality, his reflexes sharper and more responsive than they'd ever been.

Autoinjector.

There were only two shots left. He'd thought it would only be him and Luca that needed neutralisation. He didn't want to be like this forever. And if Ivan had survived, by tomorrow night he'd be at the man's mercy.

'Be prepared to fire if they come at us or move to attack the woman.'

Gotta get out of here.

There was no benefit waiting around for the police to arrest him. Jett figured he could only take down one enhanced person at a time. *If I can neutralise Gen and get Luca away, maybe I can even up the odds.*

Digging into his pocket, he fisted one of the

autoinjectors and ran at Gen. Keeping it hidden so neither Luca nor Gen could guess his intentions, he used his superior reflexes to dodge the man's attack as he launched at his target.

'Don't shoot, don't shoot.'

By keeping Gen in the line of fire, he'd effectively prevented the police from taking him out. Within striking distance, he watched her eyes luminesce in readiness for his attack. Confident he could get around her self-defence skills, he pulled out the injector, removed the lid, and feigned a hit to her head with his other hand. Instead of head contact, he drove the automatic injector towards her thigh, but at the last instant she pirouetted away, into a sprint. The injector swished through the air into nothing, putting him off balance. *Man!*

Recovering his steps, he recapped the injector. While Gen sped off into the darkness like a self-propelled missile, he shouted, 'Can't keep up with me, can you, lying Luca?' Shoving the autoinjector back in his pocket, he started running in the opposite direction, towards the Bayside Parklands. If anything went down, he wanted to ensure Luca was as far away from humanity, and Gen, as possible. The augmented man's roar indicated he was close behind.

Chapter 15

Wind tussled Jett's hair as he ran faster than he could imagine. It felt amazing. Buildings snapped past like sketches on a page, eventually giving way to bushland. Still, he didn't slow. If this was only partial enhancement, what would he be capable of in a few hours?

He didn't know if this was normal, or whether taking three capsules at once had accelerated the effect. The scent of eucalyptus and other native trees infused his nostrils as he sprinted into the darkened brush. It was then he realised his mistake. The darker the surrounds, the easier it was to see him glowing.

'Oh, Jetto, there's no camouflaging here,' Luca sing-songed. 'Time to have this out.'

Jett pivoted about-face and found Luca a few metres away. 'Luca, stop. Ivan's using you.'

'That's how little *you* know,' he mocked, taking up an attacking posture. Jett mirrored this stance.

As Luca charged, Jett sidestepped at the last minute, leaving Luca tumbling face first into the dirt. He paused as the sound of an engine thundered in the sky. At first, he thought it was one of the many passenger flights that passed near that area towards the Brisbane airport, but a thumping rhythm grew more distinct. Helicopter. Had the police located them already?

The sound drowned out the footsteps behind him and Jett cratered as Luca took his legs out from under him. Wrestling free, he again took up a defensive stance. The beating blades got closer and closer, until the helicopter hovered over them, spotlight focussed on the clearing where they brawled.

Trees flailed back and forth under the powerful downdraft generated by the rotating propeller. Jett pinpointed the nearing aircraft as dust plumed into the air around him. Despite the blinding spotlight, his super-vision homed in on a figure leaning out the open side door. Ivan.

Was that a military chopper? Surely Ivan hadn't already initiated his plan? *How did he find us?* Then Jett picked out something in Ivan's hand. The controller box.

The helicopter settled on the ground a short distance from them. Small rocks and dirt sprayed out from the landing zone, riddling Jett's skin. As the engine shut down, Ivan jumped out and approached the place where he and Luca were facing off. This proved enough of a distraction to shift Luca's focus.

'I see you've joined us, Jett.' He laughed ominously.

'Not your business, Van,' Luca snarled. 'How'd you find us?'

Ivan didn't even look at Luca as he continued speaking. 'By your presentation you must have taken three at once, foolish boy. This means in a short time you'll be *all* mine.'

Jett gulped. What had he done? Clearly a concentrated hit changed the effects and the timeframe to enable mind control. Luca stiffened and Jett saw a quizzical tilt of his brow.

'What does *that* mean, Van?'

Ivan laughed. 'Such low-hanging fruit, Luca. You wanted to master your world by gaining immeasurable power, but you were giving yourself to me, *including* complete traceability.'

Luca marched up to Ivan and reached to grip his throat. With a click of a button, Ivan commanded, 'Luca, stop.' Luca paused mid-action.

'Quite the unexpected cost. Yes? You see, your strength is linked to another mechanism that opens a pathway enabling me to control your desires, your thoughts, your actions—even your memories, if I want.'

Tilting his head, rooster-like, his eyes mocked the frozen man. 'You did one thing right, though. You *finally* brought me the prize—a young man with self-control unrivalled by most.'

Jett backed into the bushland as Ivan switched his focus onto him. The man's eyes were greedy and cold, bottoming out Jett's stomach. He wondered how long before he'd lose himself to the commands of the rogue PT.

'This will be an excellent test, given you are both at similar capacity. But I think we can add another variable that will make it even *more* interesting.' A leer twisted his features as a second figure exited the aircraft.

It was Gen. *But how?* Only then did Jett comprehend Ivan must have set this up and he'd walked right into the trap. In the time it took him to get to the parklands, Gen could have easily fled straight to Ivan and his helicopter, in a prearranged location.

Her whole body radiated green, with spectrums of pulsing colour. Ivan must have given her another dose. Given she'd obviously taken one to reactivate, whether by choice or not, another capsule would make four. She would be fully enhanced now.

Far out. There was no way he could beat them both. Despite his heightened senses, for the first time since taking the capsules Jett felt fear coil through him. As Ivan pressed the button on the controller, his calm detachment collapsed under a tidal wave of fear.

Narrowing his gaze, Van gave his orders into the box. 'Imogen, Luca, disable Jett and bring him to me. He is your enemy.'

At these words, something shifted inside Jett and he knew his control was slipping. He was certain it would be a fight to the death—Ivan would leave no witnesses—and he would soon be a human killing machine. He turned, ran, but footsteps closed in well before he'd reached the thicker scrub beyond.

He skidded about mid-stride and faced his attackers. Luca came at him first. As if he'd suddenly become a super ninja, Jett leaped and with a mid-air kick, dropped Luca to the dirt. Directly behind him was Gen. He deflected her just as effortlessly.

How on earth …? Clearly taking three capsules at once had changed the game. Significantly. Maybe even Ivan had underestimated the effects.

Flipping through the air like an elite gymnast, he landed on his feet and met their counterattack. Dodging their assaults, he peppered them with his own strikes. Over a dozen times they tried to pin him down, capture him in a headlock, kick his legs out from under him, twist his arms from their sockets, or any other means of taking him out. Nothing worked.

Jett sensed Ivan getting bored. *Gotta neutralise these two before he gets creative.* No sooner had this thought formed when his magnified hearing heard Ivan change the command.

'Imogen, I gave you a gun. Take it and kill yourself. Luca, restrain Jett.'

A flash radiated from Jett's skin, betraying his spike of panic.

'Imogen, no!' he shouted, but his distraction enabled Luca the upper hand. Before Jett could fend him away, Luca had him in a headlock.

Struggling for air, he clawed at Luca's arm. The man was like a Pitbull terrier with a bone. He watched as Gen pulled a gun from the band of her shorts, just metres from where he and Luca struggled. His head started to drift for lack of oxygen. It had taken longer, but apparently he could still die. His neck vertebrae popped as Luca cinched his hold tighter.

Gen raised the gun and placed it against her temple. *Stop. Imogen, don't do it!* Jett's mind throbbed, his pulse peaking.

'Gen, stop,' Ivan commanded, clearly enjoying the display. 'Shoot Jett. In the heart.'

Everything seemed to happen in slow motion. Really, it was milliseconds before Gen had the gun aimed at him. The muscles in her hand tensed as she squeezed the trigger. At this instant he pivoted hard, flipping Luca into the firing line. But Gen didn't stop with one shot. She was intent on hitting her mark.

Luca flailed and roared as bullets punctured his body. With this, he loosened his hold, leaving Jett gasping for air as Imogen emptied the magazine. Instead of disabling Luca, it seemed this wounding only enraged him more.

Jett could hear Ivan giving orders, telling both Imogen and Luca to capture him, but Luca was beyond control. With a sky-rupturing scream, Luca's body emitted so much light Jett had to shield his eyes. Dark liquid leaked from holes in Luca's back and side as he charged across the clearing, towards Ivan.

Jett saw the whites of Ivan's eyes, even at that distance. Shouted commands had no effect as Ivan scrambled into the helicopter and closed the door to protect himself from his crazed pursuant.

The muffled commands continued, but they were drowned out by the flat thump of Imogen colliding into Jett's body. Unprepared for this assault, he coiled to the ground. There was no playing around this time as she applied every fighting technique she knew. Jett didn't stand a chance.

Throwing himself at her, he locked his arms around her arms and torso, reducing the force of her hits. 'Imogen, please. It's Jett. You said you didn't want to kill me.' Nothing was getting through.

He had no options left and the seemingly indomitable strength of his empowered muscles was giving way to fatigue. Face aligned with hers, he did the only thing he could think of. He bent his head and kissed her in the same way she had kissed him at the bay.

Gen exhaled a small breath and her mouth moulded to his, but there was no invitation in the angle of her head. To further distract her, Jett released his arm lock on her torso and gripped the thickness of her braids with one hand. When tension thinned her lips into hard lines, he pre-empted her counterattack. As she pitched back, he plunged his other hand into his pocket to secure an autoinjector. His hold on her head was also restricting one of her arms, so he anticipated the defensive move this triggered. This enabled just enough time for him to wrench the autoinjector from his pocket, uncap it with his teeth, and arrow it into her thigh.

As he did this, police cars flooded the scene and formed a secured perimeter. Though they maintained a reasonable distance, their headlights nearly blinded him. In moments, Gen gasped and went lax in his arms.

'Imogen?' Her trembling rivalled a violent earthquake. He locked his arms around her, as if this could contain the shattered fragments of the reality imposed upon her.

A muted scream wrenched through Gen as she anchored her arms around his neck. 'I'm so sorry, Jett. I remember what happened at the waterfront now. He changed my memories, my thoughts. I can't believe what I just did.'

All he wanted to do was hold her close until every last tremor left her body, but just beyond the police perimeter, Luca was tearing off the helicopter door like it was aluminium foil. While directives echoed from a loud hailer, Jett released Gen and turned towards the helicopter. 'Stay here. I've got to deal with Luca and Ivan.'

'Jett, wait.' Her voice fractured as she was forced to release him. 'Ivan has another dose. You need to get it off him.'

But he was already turning away. Fisting the last autoinjector from his pocket, he uncapped it and sprinted towards Luca.

A strange darkness thickened about him as he

neared the enraged, luminescing man. Even as Jett pulled back his hand and snapped the injector into Luca's shoulder, he felt like his body had been dropped into resin. Grinding to a halt, he was barely aware of Luca curling over on the ground. Turning his attention to Ivan, his mind closed up like a newly constructed brick wall.

Chapter 16

Ivan's mouth twisted into a cruel sneer. '*Finally.*' Lifting the control box, he clicked the button and gave his command. 'Jett, kill Luca and Imogen. They are your enemies.'

Ivan's voice was like an electrical pulse deep in his brain. Somehow the box converted the words to a specific wavelength that bypassed audible command. His mind screamed for him to reject this order, his body spasming in resistance, but his muscled obeyed. *God, help me!*

Gripping Luca by the arms, he picked the bleeding man off the ground and hurled him against the side of the helicopter like a wet towel. Luca's body connected with a sickening smack and he slid, unmoving, to the ground.

'Jett, no!' Imogen's cry crossed the distance between them. 'Ivan, leave him alone.'

Ivan laughed. 'Finish him, then kill Imogen. You must leave no survivors.'

Inside Jett was breathless with horror. Was Luca really dead? Had he just murdered a man? No matter how much he disliked Luca, he had no desire to end his life. It was like watching someone else commit atrocities, and yet, his own hands were enacting the crime. No matter how hard he fought, he couldn't regain control.

Numb inside, he gathered Luca up by the neck and started crushing the man's windpipe. A voice sounded behind him.

'Let him go, Jett.'

He wanted to listen to Gen's directive, but he couldn't stop. His hands twitched with attempted resistance. Ivan laughed again. The police began closing in.

'You resist well, young Jett, but I've changed my mind. Kill Imogen. She is your enemy.'

He moaned in anguish as he released Luca's limp form and faced her. *Gen, I'm sorry.*

'Jett, Imogen has a gun, remember? Get it off her, reload it with these, and shoot her. Ensure the police see you do it.' He handed Jett a fresh magazine of bullets. 'When you've killed Imogen, run home and kill your family using the same gun. If you run out of bullets, strangle them to finish the job. Don't let anyone stop you.'

No! Not my family.

He had no more antidote injectors. Nothing could change him back. Only death could stop him. Although his body couldn't show it, inside his emotions were being sawn to pieces with a blunt knife. Grief pulled on him like a heavy-duty resistance band. Shaking violently, he fought Ivan's command, giving Imogen time to escape. Instead of running away, she came closer.

Gen, run. Don't come near me. But she continued to approach with her head up, eyes locked on his.

'Jett, I've got the gun.' She kept a hand on the weapon stashed at her waistband. She seemed irrationally calm as she stood just out of reach. 'But I'm not giving it to you. It's going to be okay.'

Sharp pains of regret stabbed inside him as she stood, feet set slightly apart, knees bent. It was as if—

Before he could react, Imogen leaped the short distance to Ivan and kicked him so hard he fell back into the chopper, through the opening that gaped from Luca's attack. Blood trickled from Ivan's mouth as he clutched the remote control to his lips.

'Shoot her, then shoot your family,' he roared, even as Imogen kicked the device from his hands, sending it flying into the darkened scrubland surrounding them. Her next kick rendered Ivan unconscious.

With lightning speed, Jett lunged forward and snatched the weapon from the band of her shorts. Removing the spent magazine, he replaced it with the new one in a flash. Somehow, he knew what to do. In seconds the gun was pointed at Imogen's head. Distantly, a loudhailer-enhanced voice demanded he put the gun down.

Imogen turned and faced him. 'Jett, if you shoot me, I know you can't help it. But if you could just hold on while I get something from Ivan ...' Her words wobbled like a child walking in stilettos. 'Can you resist long enough for me to do that?'

In his head Jett screamed at himself to lower the firearm. The trust in Imogen's eyes was overwhelming as she stepped back and crouched beside Ivan's unconscious form. Jett's whole body writhed as he desperately resisted squeezing the trigger.

Closing his eyes, he ground his teeth and moaned, but nothing could stop the inevitable.

'Jett, another second and I can h—'

The gunshot obliterated her plea. He opened his eyes as her body flew backwards and tumbled to the floor of the helicopter, next to Ivan.

Hot tears leaked from his eyes as he turned and sprinted through the bushland, away from the police blockading the road. His enhanced hearing detected a cry for help. Gen? But he knew it couldn't be.

Running at high speed felt effortless, but his newfound capacity was a curse as he neared his house even faster than he'd imagined. Festive Christmas lights blinked on and off as he ran down suburban streets. The festivities celebrating the birth of the Christ child mocked his assignment of death.

He'd hoped putting distance between him and the controller—wherever it had landed—would release him from the powerful compulsion, but Ivan's orders still drove him. Throwing open the yard gate, he stepped up onto the portico of their new home and used his key to unlock the front door. Pushing it open with a soft creak, he walked inside.

Everything in him screamed 'run away'. Around him the house stood silent, as if holding its breath. Leaving the door ajar, he moved forward against his will, his steps sure and determined. Despite the hot, humid evening, and his extreme physical exertion, he was barely breaking a sweat. He whimpered as he entered the hall and approached the first bedroom. Anna.

Quaking as he fought Ivan's orders, he heard a car pull up outside the house. He prayed it was the neighbours, but knew it was most likely Mum and Dad returning from their night out.

God, don't let me do this. Stop me—somehow. Protect my family. He pleaded silently as he tried to resist. Within moments he was standing over his baby sister's bed.

His body lit up the room—a real life ghoul from the realm of nightmares. The bedclothes were in a tangled mound heaped up over Anna's face and body, as if she'd been wrestling in her sleep. A tuft of blonde hair fanned across the pillow from under the sheet, her face covered by her cat-print coverlet. *Better that way.*

Sirens wailed background to his silent battle, but abruptly ceased. Tears dripped down his face as he aimed the weapon at the lump where her head rested under the bedclothes. Convulsive resistance could not negate the impossible mental siege driving his actions. Teeth gritted, his weakness for Gen paled to nothing against this force.

Quick footsteps sounded in his ears, coming nearer with each second. Soon he sensed a presence near Anna's door, but was compelled to complete what he started. *Mum and Dad shouldn't have to see this.* Worse, he knew as soon as Anna was dead, he'd turn and shoot them too.

A female voice cried out behind him as he squeezed

the trigger. The gunshot blast breached his solar plexus like a boxer's blow. A shriek burst from the direction of Sophie's room. *Soph, don't come, don't—* Immediately someone was at his back. Pivoting to deflect them, a pinpoint stabbed his rhomboid muscle and the room began to swirl, like he was being sucked down a whirlpool.

As if a giant fist had released him, the constricting restraint he'd experienced dropped away and he crumpled to his knees, exhausted. Great, heaving sobs broke from the recesses of his gut as he threw himself across the bed covers. 'Anna!' Throat closing over, it sounded like he was being choked. *I love you more than you'll ever know.*

Arms came about him and a voice whispered near his ear. 'It's okay, Jett. It's over.'

Imogen? He scrambled about-face on his knees and staggered to his feet. *Nothing* was okay. 'I thought you were dead.' He took in the blood smattering her shirt and jaw, then located the red-stained surgical dressing taped to her deltoid.

Eyes brimming, she shook her head. 'Just a surface wound and some good acting. They patched me up on the way here.'

Stricken, Jett turned back to the bed with a

despairing moan. He gagged, close to throwing up. Imogen's arms crept around him from behind and locked across his chest.

'I'm so sorry I didn't get here sooner.' Her breath dusted the back of his neck, her words feather soft, as if she understood his pain. 'The police drove me here as fast as they could. I knew Ivan had the last autoinjector on him, which I took back as he was arrested. He snatched it from my bag when he and Luca reactivated me.'

Jett rasped a palm across his face as he mustered the courage to pull back the covers, but a shrieking form flew at him from across the hall.

'Anna?' His voice broke as his little sister slammed into him and encircled his waist with her arms, pushing Imogen back. He swung her fluidly into his arms. Gen discreetly took the gun from his hand and pocketed it. Sophie followed fast on Anna's heels, flicking on the bedroom light as she entered.

Jett was momentarily dazzled by the brightness. He blinked, bringing his twin's whitened features into focus.

'Anna, I said to stay with ... Jett?' Sophie's voice pitched up in uncertainty, but Anna's words barrelled over her.

'I had a nightmare, Jett. Someone was trying to hurt you. It scared me so much. Sophie let me stay in her bed.' Emotion distorted the young girl's words.

Forcing an appearance of calm, Jett took a shuddering breath and tightened his hold on her. 'Me too, Anna. An awful nightmare.' His twin narrowed her gaze as two armed police officers blocked the doorway of the room. Ignoring them, he captured his sister's eye. 'Thanks, Soph.'

'What's going on, Jett? Imogen?' she asked, unable to disguise the fear thinning her voice. 'It sounded like a … I–I didn't know whether to hide or … Well, when Anna heard your voice, she ran in here.' Her gaze shifted to the police observing the scene, her fingers knotting at her waist.

Taking this cue, the police re-holstered their guns. 'There was a disturbance in the area and we were worried you might have been … affected.'

Understanding cleared her eyes. She nodded and glanced at Anna, still latched onto Jett like a terrified monkey. 'Right. I guess you two need to go with the police to … help them?'

'We do.' Imogen nodded. 'Thanks for understanding, Sophie. Let's go, Jett.'

Jett watched as Gen backed towards the door and unobtrusively passed the handgun to one of the officers.

'Anna, Jett's got to help the police,' Sophie reassured their sister. 'He'll be home later.'

Anna reluctantly loosened her hold, allowing Jett to set her down. She quirked her head at her brother, then his friend. 'Is Imogen your girlfriend?'

Jett choked on a breath. 'No, Anna, Imogen's not my girlfriend, but she's pretty much my guardian angel.'

Frowning, Anna turned her attention to her bed and flung back the covers. The mound that had looked like her sleeping, was actually her collection of toys tangled up in her coverlet. The long strands of blonde-hair spreading over the pillowcase, trailed from a doll. 'Why's there a hole in my dolly's head?' She picked up the doll. 'And my pillow?'

Jett gave a nervous laugh and his eyes darted to Gen, then the police. 'It's nothing. Sophie can help patch up your doll and get you a new pillow, right Soph?' *And sheets. And mattress ...* 'Tell Mum and Dad I'll be home later.'

Chapter 17

Jett finished his last bench press and switched places with his training buddy to spot his final set.

'Whoa, Jett, you're kicking butt, dude. I should ask your sister to help me with *my* training plan. I've never seen anyone bulk and shred like you have in such a short time.'

Jett gave a measured smile as the guy removed forty kilos off the bar and lay on the bench. He didn't have the heart to say he could have easily lifted twice the weight he had.

This was his first training session since the weekend of hell, the first day he'd finished work early enough to feel up to facing a workout. Dark gyms gave him the creeps these days. Despite his lack of enthusiasm, no matter what he attempted, his capacity remained significantly enhanced since ingesting Ivan's performance modifier.

They had moved through their sets, drawing more attention from other gym members who stopped to appreciate his rapid progression. But Jett felt like a cheat. To escape the attention, he'd all but decided to forgo the final accessory exercises of his routine.

'Thought I'd find you here.'

Gen. Though Jett kept his attention on his training partner, his heart gave a sharp, distracting kick. For once, her braids were their natural russet brown and hanging loose down her back. Taking in her flowing skirt and fitted top, it was a far cry from the gym gear she usually wore, and amped up her classiness another notch. 'Hey.'

'Hey, Jett.'

He looked to the guy now towelling sweat off his face. 'I'm done—thanks, buddy. I'll see you next time.'

Imogen folded her arms and smiled. 'You know, if you've got a few minutes, I could go another one of those ice creams at the waterfront.'

Glancing at Gen, he allowed himself a half smile, but tried to play it smooth. 'I've gotta pick up Soph from the lab where she's doing a summer placement after this, and I'm hoping to catch my best mate along the way. But if you give me a few mins to clean up, we can do that.'

'Sounds good. I'll wait in the foyer.'

Jett tried not to show how she affected him as

they walked from the weight area. Given his face was now a furnace and he'd just tripped on his own towel, he knew the only person he was fooling was himself. A glance betrayed her face lit with amusement, making his chest grow warm and buoyant.

Finally, he made it to the locker room without walking into a wall. Soon he'd showered and changed. He located Imogen and together they headed for his car.

Jett put his kit in the back and closed the hatch. 'How's Luca?'

'Still a jerk, but he'll live. Can't believe that many bullets didn't kill him. They penetrated, but the tissue damage and blood loss was remarkably minimal.' She closed her eyes, hugged herself, and shuddered. 'Jett, I … I can't stop seeing what I did.'

He blew out a breath and dug his fists into his pockets. 'Yeah. I know what you mean. I tried so hard not to …' He gulped, his insides sinking.

She reached out and rested her hand on his forearm. 'Don't. I understand.' Her touch set off an internal blaze. 'Let's just do ice cream—my shout this time, so long as you don't mind driving me? I came in an Uber.'

'No problem.'

'And so you're not late for your sister, how 'bout

we go to the waterfront near your house? I'll grab an Uber home from there. That way you can get going when you need.'

''Kay.'

They soon walked barefoot along Moreton Bay, ice creams in hand. Jett's feet made a soft squeak each time he stepped, leaving a damp, gritty, layer clinging to his soles. A light, salty breeze cleared away the sweat-tinted remnants of gym air in his lungs.

'Good thing the police saw enough of that freak show to believe us,' he said. 'And good thing you knew Ivan had that injector.'

Imogen nodded. 'I'd planned using it on Luca, but Ivan got to it first.'

'The guy's seriously sick.' He brushed a toe across the grainy surface underfoot. 'It would've been *me* in jail for multiple murders, if he'd gotten his way. Even after he was in custody and our statements verified, for a while there I thought the police were never going to release me.'

'Not if *I* had a say in it.' She narrowed her gaze, as if daring anyone to try incarcerate him. 'Thankfully they were able to find the controller and corroborate our stories with those of the emergency services, the report from the production facility explosion, and the hospital.'

He gave an easy laugh. 'Yeah, the miraculous recovery of your broken leg sure had Senior Constable Gassmann scratching his head.'

She stopped walking and angled her chin to him, her unfettered hair dancing about her shoulders. 'So, Channing, now you're all bulked an' shredded, are you still doing that bodybuilding comp?'

Jett chewed down the last part of his waffle cone and shook his head. 'Nah, I think I'd have an unfair advantage, given all it took to get these guns was a few cacky tasting capsules. Which, by the way, you said took a *day* or so to reach robot mode.'

Imogen threw up her free hand and resumed her stroll. 'Sorry, I didn't know you'd take them all at once.'

'So long as we all got out alive, yeah?' He caught her eye as the sun leaned nearer the horizon. His statement was an uncomfortable reminder of their all-too-real brush with death.

'Did you tell your family what happened?'

He glanced up the street, towards their house. His Dad chose that moment to emerge on the deck with a drink. Jett gave him a two-fingered salute and turned back to the water. 'Not really. I mean, Sophie pulled out her finest interrogation skills, but the feds made it clear they don't want news of the incident getting out, especially given Van's infiltration of Australia's frontline defence forces. I figure blissful ignorance works best for everyone. And you? Did you tell your fam anything?'

Imogen sucked a drip of ice cream off the tip of her finger. As Jett watched, he couldn't stop his eyes catching on her lips. An all too familiar longing pulsed through him and the memory of them kissing rushed back. But her sigh that followed sucked the oxygen from his lungs.

Gen's eyes skipped towards him, then away, not quite making contact. 'I actually came to tell you I've decided to spend Christmas with my family.'

'England?' His stomach plunged, as if she'd pushed him out of a plane without a parachute.

She nodded and finished her last mouthful. 'Yeah, I leave tomorrow.'

'I understand.' He tried keeping his voice upbeat and light, but it fell flat, betraying his disappointment.

She reached out and took his hand in hers. Instantly the persistent coals of desire for her flamed to incinerator levels. 'I know it's not the greatest timing, given your nineteenth birthday's coming up. Truth is, I'm going to miss you. But after all that's happened, I need to re-ground myself.'

'At least I know at that distance you're not going

to try killing me anytime soon.' He softened the barb with a grin.

'Jett, that's not funny.' She released his hand and smacked his shoulder. 'It really freaked me out and ... and I couldn't have lived with myself if you, or even Luca, had died because of me.' All at once her lips trembled and tears glistened like diamonds in her eyes.

Jett held her gaze. 'Sorry, Gen. Believe me, the feeling's mutual. I thought my good guy persona would save me from Ivan's control. I guess I'm not as nice as I thought.'

Imogen stepped forward, closing the gap between them. Her aroma swirled over him, intoxicating his senses with crisp, clear notes of lemon, vanilla and lavender. Her nearness was dizzying.

'Jett, you're the nicest guy I know, and that's perfectly fine by me. But can I ask you something?'

'Shoot.' *Argh, wrong word choice.* But it was like his brain had put up a 'gone fishing' sign.

She paused, as if arranging the words in her mind.

'What did you mean about me "pretty much" being your guardian angel?'

'You were kinda the answer to a desperate prayer,' he admitted hoarsely, his voice rasping with emotion. Searching her eyes, as if memorising each grey-to-tawny fractal, he added, 'I don't want to think about what would've happened if you didn't come when you did.'

Her eyes cleared and small creases smoothed from her brow. 'Well, consider this an official acceptance of your guardian angel appointment—given I apparently don't meet the criteria for *other* positions. But maybe we can explore that further, going forward.'

Jett raised his eyebrows, anticipation teeming inside him. 'Does that mean you might look me up when you're back?' He was acutely aware of the warmth emanating between them.

Imogen leaned into him, eyes crinkling with the widening of her smile. 'That could be a *distinct* possibility—even if I'm *not* your girlfriend ... yet.' She laughed lightly and circled his neck with her arms, like a human lei Jett never wanted to remove.

He grinned and placed his hands at her waist. 'You do realise guardian angel's a pretty high-level role? But you never know, promotion to girlfriend could be a career move down the road.'

Gen's face was alight. The way she looked at him made him feel weightless, like he might float into the sky any time now. His focus was drawn to her mouth, now quirked with amusement. He bent his head near and felt the brush of her breath. All teasing vanished as Jett risked getting lost in her wide, open gaze. 'Don't forget me while you're gone, Imogen Gale.'

Her hold on him tightened, drawing them so close her lips danced with rose-petal softness against his when she spoke. 'As if.'

Pulse escalating, he didn't pull away. 'Mind if I kiss you goodbye?'

She smiled against his mouth. 'Thought you'd never ask.'

About the Author

'Science fiction for the real world.'

Australian author, Adele Jones, writes young adult fringe, science-fantasy and near-science fiction that explores the underbelly of bioethics and confronting teen issues, including disability, self-worth, loss, domestic conflict, and more. She also writes historical fiction, poetry, inspirational non-fiction and short fictional works, with themes of social justice, humanity, faith, natural beauty and meaning in life's journey. Adele's first YA novel *Integrate* (book one of the Blaine Colton Trilogy) was awarded the 2013 CALEB Prize for unpublished manuscript. As a speaker she seeks to present a practical and encouraging message by drawing on themes from her writing.

To find out more visit www.adelejonesauthor.com

Acknowledgements

Stories do not arise in a vacuum and I am grateful for Anne Hamilton's editing prowess during the creative process of *Flare Up*. Incredible work by Kirsten Hart on the cover design—love it so much! Much appreciation to Jeanette O'Hagan and Rebekah Robinson for answering my many "I'm freaking out here" questions and messages during this first indie publication journey. I know the book isn't perfect, but it's 100 times better because of your input. To my loyal readers, there has not been a story you have requested more than Jett's. So, this one's for you. I still recommend reading *Replicate* with a box of tissues, but it is my hope this novella will provide a deeper dive into the behind-the-scenes adventures of this well-loved character from the Blaine Colton trilogy. (Who would have imagined what Jett was getting up to, right?!) I refer to this story as book 1.5, given it sits between the end of *Integrate* and leans into the first half of *Replicate*, and I hope you enjoy reading it as much as I enjoyed writing it. And as Jett says, always remember you are known and loved.

HAVE YOU READ

SIGNAL ERASED?

SIGNAL ERASED ISBN: 978-1-76111-143-3

Anna Faraday's carefully ordered world comes crashing down when her gift of singing is turned against in a secret frequency-based experiment that alters her atomic state. Unseen and unheard, she seeks help from the last guy she ever thought she'd ask. Will he, or anyone, understand what's happened before she disappears forever?

www.wombatrhiza.com.au/signal-erased

OR THE SERIES THAT STARTED IT ALL?

INTEGRATE (2ND EDITION) ISBN: 978-1-76111-011-5
BOOK ONE IN THE BLAINE COLTON TRILOGY

Blaine Colton has already fought and won his battle with genetic disease, but now he's in the clutches of an ambitious medical researcher who tells him his revolutionary gene therapy was never approved. Locked up and denied access to his family and the medication keeping him alive, he is running out of time to find answers before his ultimate fear is realised—returning to a state where all he can do is "be".

www.wombatrhiza.com.au/integrate